My Favourite
Escape
Stories

Edited by P. R. Reid, M.B.E., M.C.

Beaver Books

First published in this collected form in 1975 by
Lutterworth Press
Luke House, Farnham Road, Guildford, Surrey, England

This paperback edition published in 1977 by
The Hamlyn Publishing Group Limited
London . New York . Sydney . Toronto
Astronaut House, Feltham, Middlesex, England

© Copyright Introduction P. R. Reid 1975
© Copyright Introductory and concluding passages and
editorial links within episodes P. R. Reid 1975
ISBN 0 600 36281 7

Printed in England by
Hazell Watson & Viney Limited, Aylesbury, Bucks
Set in Monotype Baskerville

My Favourite Escape Stories

Major Pat Reid's favourite escape stories of four hundred years range from the Tower of London in 1597 to Shanghai in 1944. Whether imprisoned in fortress, POW camp, transport ship or slave plantation, the men and women in these stories all share an immense skill and determination and a 'courage beyond most men's powers'. Major Reid, who himself broke out of Colditz Castle in 1942, is the author of many books. The best known is 'The Colditz Story', which became a popular TV series. He now lives and farms in Sussex.

Acknowledgements

The editor and the publishers are indebted to all those who have given permission for the use of material which is their copyright, or have helped in the obtaining of that permission:

The Longman Group Limited, for 'The Escape of Father John Gerard', taken from *The Hunted Priest*, the Autobiography of John Gerard, translated by Philip Caraman, S.J. (Longmans, Green & Co. Ltd, 1951)

Mr Jack D. Jones, of Carisbrooke Castle Museum, and Lutterworth Press, for 'The Attempted Escape of Charles I', taken from *The Royal Prisoner* by Jack D. Jones (Lutterworth Press, 1965)

The Council of the Scottish History Society, for 'The Escape of Stewart Carmichael', taken from *The Lyon in Mourning* by the Revd Robert Forbes (Scottish History Society), and the Trustees of the National Library of Scotland as owners of the original manuscript from which the Society published the texts

The Bodley Head, for 'The Escape of Lieutenant J. L. Hardy', taken from *I Escape!* by J. L. Hardy (Bodley Head)

Edward Arnold (Publishers) Ltd, for 'The Escape of Captain M. C. C. Harrison and Lieutenant H. A. Cartwright', taken from *Within Four Walls* by M. C. C. Harrison and H. A. Cartwright (Edward Arnold & Co., 1930)

Acknowledgements

The British Broadcasting Corporation, for 'The Attempts of Oberleutnant H. H. E. Justus to Escape from Imprisonment in England', broadcast by them on 18th July, 1931, and subsequently included in *Escapers All* by J. Ackerley (Bodley Head, 1932); the editor and publishers regret that attempts to trace Oberleutnant Justus and his family have so far proved unsuccessful, and that they are accordingly unable also to offer the customary acknowledgements to himself or his estate; they would welcome the opportunity to do so in accordance with usual practice and at the current recommended Society of Authors rate

William Blackwood & Sons Ltd, for 'The Escape of Captains Johnston, Yearsley, Ellis, Haig, Grant, Clarke and Harris, and Lieutenant-Commander Cochrane, R.N.', taken from *450 Miles to Freedom* by M. A. B. Johnston and K. D. Yearsley (William Blackwood)

Hamish Hamilton Ltd, for 'The Escape of the Tchernavin Family', taken from *Escape from the Soviets* by Tatiana Tchernavin (Hamish Hamilton, 1933)

The Estate of A. J. Evans, and A. P. Watt & Son, for 'The Escape of Wing-Commander Basil Embry, R.A.F.', taken from *Escape and Liberation* by A. J. Evans (Hodder & Stoughton, 1945)

Hodder and Stoughton Ltd, for 'The Escape of Lieutenant Pierre Mairesse Lebrun', taken from *The Colditz Story* by P. R. Reid (Hodder & Stoughton, 1952)

O. L. S. Philpot, Esq. for 'The Escape of Flight Lieutenant O. L. S. Philpot, R.A.F.V.R.', taken from *Stolen Journey* (Hodder & Stoughton)

Acknowledgements

The Estate of the late Quentin Reynolds, and Random House Inc., for 'The Escape of Lieutenant-Commander C. D. Smith, U.S.N.R.', taken from *Officially Dead* by Quentin Reynolds (Cassell & Co. Ltd, U.K., and Random House Inc., U.S.A.; copyright 1945 and renewed 1973 by James J. Reynolds and Frederick H. Rohlfs)

William Kimber & Co. Ltd, for 'The Escapes of Oberleutnant Franz von Werra', taken from *Single or Return?* by Fritz Wentzel (William Kimber & Co.)

The editor and the publishers are also grateful to the following for their generous help with the obtaining and checking of material: Commander G. P. B. Naish, R.N.R., of the Society for Nautical Research; the British Library Board; the Imperial War Museum, London; the National Maritime Museum, Greenwich; and the Naval Historical Center and the Headquarters of the United States Marine Corps, Department of the Navy, Washington, U.S.A.

Contents

Contents

To
the escapers of the future,
those who try but fail
as well as those who succeed,

Introduction

The escape of the mind from the realities of living is practised either sedulously or haphazardly by everyone who reads books. Books provide an escape. Books written literally about the art and techniques of escaping from an enemy who has imprisoned you, are only a specific section of the enormous world library of escape. You do not escape from yourself or from reality more by reading specifically books from the escapology section of this great library. On the contrary you will almost certainly tend to be brought face to face with your real self. So that, far from 'Escape stories' being any escape for you, they may well become the opposite; they are more likely to bring you to judgement; to put you in the dock; to try you. Therein lies their fascination.

I think that the majority of readers of 'Escape stories' deliberately put themselves on trial. They want to search their own hearts to find out whether they, too, possess those characteristics which we so lovingly and admiringly attribute to the hunted animal who succeeds in eluding his bloodthirsty pursuers. Such attributes appear, from time immemorial, to be considered wholesome and good. We love the wily old fox who has survived many a gruelling hunt. May I, even, be forgiven for hinting at the grudging admiration we are tempted to bestow upon the criminal who has escaped from his gaolers!

This self-examination by the reader is, of course, brought about by what we call identification with the subject, more particularly with the actual escaper or 'hero' of the story. Now that most famous of all 'escape' stories, *The Count of Monte Cristo*, is fiction, so I ask myself, do we have this same sense of identification with the Count as with the hero of a true escape story? M. Dumas writes so well that I think we are hoodwinked. In fact, I have met several people who believed the Count of Monte Cristo was a historical character.

Escape stories, to become my favourites, must be factual and unadorned. I think this provides a deeper fascination for the reader. He is not testing himself against a fictitious nor even a real hero in exaggerated situations. He is dealing with just another man placed in a most distressing predicament.

I find myself drawn and attracted to the unvarnished truth which shines through a story. I think I can discern when the story-teller begins slipping from the straight and narrow path. I hope the reader will subscribe to this – my first criterion; that the situation of complete identification can be achieved in a story that is completely true.

Beyond this I must admit that I am drawn irresistibly by a story of courage, beyond most men's powers. I believe the quintessence of courage is possessed by an escaper who has that power within him to contemplate, select, prepare for and execute a plan that he knows beforehand must make him a target for death. Such an escape was that of Pierre Mairesse Lebrun from Colditz. To contemplate the risk beforehand in the loneliness of a solitary confinement cell would be enough to daunt the boldest. To continue in the endeavour and subject the cowardly body to the domination of a courageous will, while training for the event; then finally to execute it, running the gauntlet of bullets, surpasses for me even the courage that earns Victoria Crosses in the heat of mortal conflict.

Most successful escapes contain an element of originality in their execution. This aspect is endearing. In fact it has caused me great heartsearching in selecting my short list of favourites. So many original escape attempts start off with dramatic good luck on the side of the escapers only to end in bitter misfortune. The combination of superb originality crowned with complete success is so rare that it makes history. The Wooden Horse escape is one of these.

In the category of successful originality I have reluctantly to forego the inclusion of entertaining sections of the story from the book, *The Road to Endor*. This saga of an English Officer and an Australian Officer, prisoners of war in Yozgad, Turkey, during the First World War, relates how they convinced the Turkish Camp Commandant that they were in communication with the Spirit World. He connived at their removal from prison to search for a hidden treasure. The plot is ingenious and intricate and alas! its subtlety and impact would be lost by the abbreviation which the length of this story would entail.

I am intrigued by historical escapes; the daring efforts of men and women who risked torture and death for freedom, long before we had the Geneva Convention to temper the cruelty of enemies who had the power to kill or let live their prisoners at their whim. I have gone back as far as the sixteenth century and selected seven stories up to the twentieth century.

I was seriously tempted to include more stories from the Jacobite rebellion of '45, particularly as my research worker and editor, Miss Jenny Overton, discovered that five prisoners escaped from Edinburgh Castle which was considered the safest prison in Scotland, if not in the whole United Kingdom, with a strong garrison and a stern governor. The five should be named at least. They were: Margaret Lady Ogilvie, James McKay, Thomas Ogilvie who was killed in the attempt, Alexander Reid of Aberdeen, and of Lord Pitsligo's Horse, and Peter Reid, a merchant of Perth. The latter two appear to have escaped together, being the first to make the break successfully, on 16th April, 1746. In an effort to locate a Patrick Reid, Miss Overton discovered one, imprisoned in Stirling Castle. However, he did not escape, but was released under the general pardon of 1747!

The historical escape stories have given me the opportunity to include passages concerning the conditions of imprisonment in those days. Reading of the conditions makes understandable the laconic comments of historians when recording, of so many battles, that 'no quarter was given or taken'. The alternative of imprisonment hardly bore consideration by the vanquished.

Finally, I think the reader may be impressed by the faith of so many successful escapers, who, writing in the first person, give thanks to the Almighty for their deliverance, implying their belief in his divine guidance to safety.

The work involved in compiling this book entailed the reading of many escape stories. For the benefit of a reader who may make the subject his hobby or study, I have compiled a list of titles which has been photocopied and is available on application to the hardback publishers, at Luke House, Farnham Road, Guildford, if accompanied by a large stamped and addressed envelope.

P. R. Reid.

March, 1975
Sussex

I

The Escape of Father John Gerard, S.J., the hunted Jesuit priest, from the Tower of London, 4th October, 1597

*Father John Gerard S.J. landed secretly in England in Novem-
ber, 1588, to join the English mission. His three priest-com-
panions were all subsequently captured and martyred. Gerard was
taken prisoner in the spring of 1594, questioned, tortured, and
imprisoned in the Tower of London.*

It was the last day of July [1597] and the feast of our
blessed Father.* I was making my meditation and was
longing to have the opportunity of saying Mass again,
when the thought suddenly came to me – I might be
able to do it in the cell of a Catholic gentleman in the
tower opposite me. There was only a garden between his
cell and mine.†

He had been in prison there for ten years and lay
under sentence of death, but the sentence had not yet
been carried out. Every day he used to go up on to the
lead roof above his cell where he was allowed to walk up

* *St Ignatius, the founder of the Society of Jesus. He was beatified on
27th July, 1609, the year in which J.G. was writing. He was not canonised
until 12th March, 1622.*

† *This was John Arden, who was imprisoned in the Cradle Tower which
was at the opposite corner of the Queen's Privy Garden. He was arrested
in January 1587 for alleged complicity in the Babington Plot.*

and down for exercise. From there he used to greet me and wait on his knees for my blessing.

When I turned the idea over in my mind later, I thought it might be done, if only the warder could be persuaded to let me go over. The gentleman's wife was allowed to visit him on fixed days and bring him clean linen and other things he needed. She carried them in a basket, and as she had now been doing this for years the warders had got out of the way of examining its contents. With her help I hoped we might be able little by little to bring in everything we needed for Mass. My friends, of course, would supply them.

I decided to try. So I signed to the gentleman to watch the gestures I was going to make – I dared not call to him because it was a good distance across and I might easily be overheard. He watched me as I took a pen and paper and pretended to write; next, I placed the letter over the coal fire and held it up in my hands as though I were reading it; then I wrapped up one of my crosses in it, and went through the motions of despatching it to him. He seemed to follow what I was trying to indicate.

The next step was to get the warder to take one of my crosses or rosaries to my good fellow-prisoner – the same man had charge of us both. At first he refused, saying that he could not risk it as he had no proof that the other man could be trusted to keep the secret.

'If the man said something to his wife and it became known, it would be all up with me,' he said.

But I put heart into him and told him that this was most improbable. Then I placed some money in his hand as I always did, and he agreed. My letter was taken and delivered, but the gentleman wrote nothing back as I had asked him to do. The next day, when he came out for his walk on the roof, he thanked me by signs, holding up in his hands the cross I had sent him.

When at the end of three days he had not replied I

began to suspect the reason for it. So I went through the whole series of signs again with greater precision, showing him how I squeezed the juice out of an orange and dipped my pen into the juice; and then, to bring out the writing, held the paper to the fire. This time he understood and held my next letter to the fire and read it. In his reply he said that the first time he thought I wanted him to burn the paper, because I had scribbled a few words in pencil on it, and he had done this.

He answered my query, saying he thought the scheme was practicable, provided the warder allowed me to visit him in the evening and stay over the whole of the following day; his wife would bring all the Mass requisites that were given her.

I fixed the day for the feast of the Nativity of Our Blessed Lady.* In the meantime I arranged for the prisoner's wife to go to a certain place in the city. There she would meet John Lillie, who, following the instructions in my letter, would hand her the things needed for Mass. I had also told Lillie to bring a number of small hosts and a pyx as I wanted to reserve the Blessed Sacrament.

When the evening arrived, I went across with my warder and stayed with the gentleman all that night and the following day. According to the promise we had made with the warder, not a word was said to the gentleman's wife.

That morning I said Mass. I felt very great consolation and I gave Communion to the noble confessor of Christ, who had been so many years without this comfort. I also consecrated twenty-two hosts and placed them in a pyx with a corporal and brought them back with me to my own cell, and renewed the divine banquet for many days afterwards with fresh relish and delight.

When I went across that evening I had no thought of

* *8th September, 1597.*

escape – I had only looked to the Lord Jesus, prefigured as our Redeemer in the ash-baked loaf of Elias, to give me the strength and courage I still needed to journey the rest of my hard way to the mountain of the Lord. But while we were passing the time of day together, it struck me how close this tower was to the moat encircling the outer fortifications, and I thought it might be possible for a man to lower himself with a rope from the roof of the tower on to the wall beyond the moat. I asked the gentleman what he thought.

'Yes, it could be done easily,' he said, 'if only we had some really good friends who were ready to run the risk of helping us.'

'We have the friends all right,' I said, 'if only the thing is practicable and really worth trying.'

'As far as I am concerned,' he said, 'I am all for attempting it. I would be much happier if I could live in hiding with my friends, and with the consolation of the sacraments and with pleasant companions, instead of passing my days like a solitary between these four walls.'

'Good,' I said. 'Now, we'll pray about it, and meanwhile I'll put the matter to my Superior and do whatever he thinks best.'

For the rest of the time we were together we discussed the details of the plan we would follow, if we decided on the attempt.

When I got back to my cell that night I wrote to my Superior through John Lillie and laid all the details of the scheme before him. Father Garnet replied that I certainly ought to attempt it, but I was not to risk my neck in the descent.

I then wrote to my former host* and told him that we were going to attempt an escape, and warned him to mention it to as few people as possible. If the plan got out, it would be all over. Then I asked John Lillie and

* *William Wiseman.*

Richard Fulwood (he was attending Father Garnet at the time) whether they were prepared to take the risk, and, if they were, to come on a certain night to the far side of the moat, opposite the squat tower I had described, near the point where Master Page had been seized. They were to bring a rope with them and tie it to a stake; we would be on the roof of the tower and throw them an iron ball attached to a stout thread, the kind used in stitching up bales. They must listen in the darkness for the sound of the ball touching the ground, find the cord and tie it to the free end of the rope. This done, we would draw up the rope by pulling the other end of the cord which we held in our hands. I told them to pin a piece of white paper or a handkerchief on the front of their jackets, for we wanted to be sure of their identity before throwing the cord. Also, they were to bring a rowing boat so that we could make a quick get-away.

When everything was arranged and the night fixed, my former host, who was afraid of the risk I was taking, was anxious that I should first see whether the warder could be bribed into letting me walk out of the prison, as I could easily do in borrowed clothes. Therefore, in the name of a friend of mine, John Lillie offered the warder a thousand florins down and a yearly allowance of a hundred florins for life. The warder would not hear of it. If he allowed it, he said, it would mean that he would be an outlaw for the rest of his life, and he would be hanged if he were caught. So the matter was dropped and we went ahead with our first plan.

I begged the earnest prayers of all who were let into the secret. One gentleman, the heir to a large estate, bound himself by vow to fast one day in the week for life, if I got away safe.

The night came. I begged and bribed my warder to let me visit my fellow-prisoner. I walked across. The warder locked the pair of us in the cell, barred the door as he always did, and went off. But he had also bolted the inside door which gave on to the stairs leading up to the roof, and we had to cut away with a knife the stone holding the socket of the bolt. There was no other way out.

At last we climbed silently up the stairs without a light, for a guard was posted every night in a garden at the foot of the wall, and when we spoke, it was in a faint whisper.

At midnight we saw the boat with our friends approaching. John Lillie and Richard Fulwood were at the oars and a third man sat at the tiller. He was my old warder in the Clink and he had obtained the boat for us. As they pulled in and got ready to land, a man came out from one of the poor dwelling-places on the bank to do something. When he saw the boat draw up, he started talking to the men, thinking they were fishermen.

He went back to bed. But the rescue party were afraid to land until the man had been given time to get to sleep again. So they paddled up and down. Time passed. It became too late to attempt anything that night.

They rowed back towards the bridge, but by now the tide had turned and was flowing strongly. It forced their little boat against the piles driven into the bed of the river to break the force of the water. It stuck, and it was impossible to move it forward or back. Meanwhile the water was rising and was striking the boat with such force that with every wave it looked as if it would capsize and the occupants be thrown into the river. They could only pray to God and shout for help.*

We were on the top of the tower and heard their shouts. Men came out on to the bank, and we were able to watch them in the light thrown by their candles. They

---

* *This was the famous old London bridge opened in 1209. It was 926 feet long and had nineteen arches buttressed by great piers, which obstructed the flow of the river.*

rushed to their boats and pulled off to the rescue. Several boats came quite near, but they were afraid to pull along-side – the current was too strong. Forming a semi-circle round them, they stayed like spectators watching the poor men in their peril without daring to assist.

Amid all the shouting I recognised Richard Fulwood's voice.

'I know it,' I said. 'It's our friends in danger.'

My companion would not believe that I could pick out anyone's voice at such a distance,* but I recognised it only too well, and I was miserable at the thought that such devoted men were in danger of their lives for my sake.

We prayed fervently for them. Though we had watched many people go out to help them, they were not saved yet. Then we saw a light lowered from the top of the bridge, and a kind of basket at the end of a rope. If only they could get into it, they could be pulled up. However, God had regard to the peril of His servants, and at last a powerful sea-going craft came along with six sailors aboard and hazardously drawing up to the craft in danger, pulled on deck Lillie and Fulwood. Then immediately the small boat capsized before the third man could be rescued – as though it had only been kept afloat for the sake of the Catholics it carried. However, by the mercy of God, the man who was washed over into the river was able to grasp the rope let down from the bridge; and he was hauled to safety.

So all were rescued and got back to their homes.

The next day John Lillie sent me a letter as usual through the warder. I might reasonably have expected him to say something like this: 'Now we know – and our peril last night has taught us – God does not want us to go ahead with the escape.' But quite the contrary. The letter began:

* *The distance was about half a mile.*

'It was not God's design that we should succeed last night, but He mercifully snatched us from our peril – He has only postponed the day. With God's help we will be back to-night.'

Determination like this and the man's devout sentiments, reassured my companion. He felt certain we would succeed. But I had great difficulty in getting leave of the warder to stay a second night out of my cell, and we were very much afraid he might notice the loosened stone when he came to bolt the door in the evening. However, he did not see it.

Meantime I had written three letters which I intended to leave behind in the cell. The first was to my warder, justifying myself for contriving my escape without letting him know. I said I was merely exercising my rights – I had committed no crime and was wrongfully held in prison. I told him I would always remember him in my prayers, if there was no other way I could help him. The purpose of this letter was to put him less at fault, in case he was imprisoned for our escape.

The second was to the Lieutenant. In this letter I made further excuses for the warder, protesting before God that he was not privy to my escape and would never have allowed it if he had known. And to prove this, I mentioned the attractive offer we had made, which he had refused. As for my going across to another cell, I had extorted his permission only with the most persistent entreaties and it would be wrong to put him to death for this.

The third letter was to the Lords of the Council. In the first place I stated my motives for regaining the freedom that was mine by right. I did it not from love of freedom for its own sake, but from love of souls – souls who were being daily lost in England. I wanted to get out and reclaim them from sin and heresy. Concerning the affairs of state they knew my clear record and could count on my not soiling it in the future. Finally, I protested and proved that neither the Lieutenant nor the warder could be charged with connivance or consent. They had known nothing about it: my escape was entirely due to my own exertions and my friends'.

I left these letters to be picked up by the warder. One last letter I wrote and took with me. It was delivered to the warder (as you shall hear) next morning – but not by John Lillie.

At the right time we went up on to the tower. The boat came along. No one interfered and it pulled in safely to the bank. The schismatic stayed in the boat, the two Catholics got out with the rope. It was a new one, as they had thrown the old into the river when they ran into trouble the previous night. Following my instructions they fastened it to a stake, and then listened for the sound of the iron ball we threw down to them. It was found without difficulty and the cord fastened to the end of the rope. But it proved very difficult indeed to pull up – it was a good deal thicker and doubled. This was Father Garnet's instructions, to guard against the rope snapping under the weight of my body. But actually he had increased the hazards.

Now a fresh difficulty arose which we had not foreseen. The distance between the tower at one end and the stake at the other was very great and the rope, instead of sloping down, stretched almost horizontally between the two points.

We had therefore to descend by working our way along the rope – it was impossible to slide down with our own weight, and this we discovered by making up a bundle of books and other things which we wrapped in my cloak and placed on the double rope to see whether it would go down of its own accord. It didn't. Fortunately, it stuck before it got out of our reach, for if it had gone beyond recovery we would never have got down ourselves. We hauled the bundle back and left it behind.*

My companion now changed his mind: he had always said it was the simplest thing in the world to slide down. Now he saw the hazards of it.

'But I shall certainly be hanged if I remain here,' he said. 'If we throw the rope back now it will fall into the moat and the splash will betray us and our friends as well. I'll go down and God help me. I'd rather take a chance of escape than stay locked up here with no chance at all.'

So he said a prayer and took hold of the rope. He got down fairly easily for he had plenty of strength and the rope was still taut. But his descent slackened the rope and made it much more difficult for me. I only noticed this when I started to descend.

I commended myself to God and Our Lord Jesus, to the Blessed Virgin, my guardian angel and especially to Father Southwell, who was imprisoned near here until he was taken out to martyrdom,† and to Father Walpole and to all our martyrs. Then I gripped the rope with my right hand, and took it in my left. To prevent myself falling I twisted my legs round the rope leaving it free to slide between my shins.

I had gone three or four yards face downwards when suddenly my body swung round with its own weight and I nearly fell. I was still very weak, and with the slack rope and my body hanging underneath I could make practically no progress. At last I managed to work myself as far as the middle of the rope, and there I stuck. My strength was failing and my breath, which was short before I started, seemed altogether spent.

* *The height of the wall beyond the moat had not been allowed for and prevented the rope inclining. As J.G. had not ventured to appear on the roof in daytime he had been unable to make an accurate reckoning.*

† *Fr Southwell was imprisoned in the Lanthorn Tower at the corner of the Queen's Privy Garden opposite the Cradle Tower.*

At last, with the help of the saints and, I think, by the power of my friends' prayers below drawing me, I moved along a little way and then I stuck again. Now I thought I would never be able to get down. But I was determined not to fall into the moat as long as I was still able to hold the rope, I tried to recover a little strength and then, using my legs and arms as well as I could, I managed, thank God, to get as far as the wall on the far side of the moat. But my feet just touched the top of the wall and the rest of my body hung horizontally behind, with my head no higher than my legs – the rope had become so slack. I don't know how I would have got over the wall, if it had not been for John Lillie. Somehow or other (he could never say how he did it), he got up on to the wall, seized hold of my feet, pulled me over and put me safely down on the ground. I could not stand upright, I was so weak. So they gave me cordial waters and restoratives which they had taken care to bring with them, and I was able to reach the boat. Before getting in they untied the rope from the stake, cut off part of it and let the rest hang down against the wall of the tower. Our first plan had been to pull it away altogether and we had accordingly passed it round a big gun on the roof without knotting it. But providentially we could not tug it loose; had we done so it would almost certainly have dropped into the moat with a big splash and we would have been in trouble.

We stepped into the boat and thanked God 'who had snatched us from the hands of our persecutors and from all the expectation of the Protestant people.' We also thanked the men who had done so much and undergone such risks for us.

Father Garnet was in the country at the time.* We rode straight to his place and had dinner with him. The

* *At a house called Morecroftes at Uxbridge.*

rejoicing was great. We all thanked God that I had escaped from the hands of my enemies in the name of the Lord.

Meanwhile I had sent Richard Fulwood to a place we had decided on beforehand, where he was to hold a horse and be ready to fly with my warder if the man was prepared to make off at once. As I said, I had written a letter to be delivered to the warder when he came for his usual morning meeting with John Lillie. But it was not Lillie who came that morning. I had ordered him not to stir out of doors until the storm that was to be expected had blown over. In his place I chose another messenger whom the warder knew. He was surprised, of course, to find another man, but he said nothing. Just as he was turning back, as he thought, to deliver the letter in his usual way, the messenger seized hold of him.

'The letter is for you; no, not for anyone else,' he said.

'For me? Who sent it?'

'A friend,' replied the other man. 'But I don't know who he is.'

The warder was dumbfounded.

'But I can't read. If it is urgent, please read it for me.'

The man read the letter he had brought. In it I informed the warder that I had escaped from prison, and, in order to put his mind at rest, briefly explained why I had done so. Then I pointed out that, though I had no obligation in the matter – I had merely made use of my rights – yet I would see to his safety. He had always been faithful in his trusts, and I would stand by him now. If he wanted to save his skin I had a man ready with a horse to take him to a safe place a good distance out of London. I would give him two hundred florins a year and he could lead a decent life. But I added this condition. If he accepted the offer he must settle his affairs in the Tower quickly and go off at once to the place to which the messenger would lead him. He was on his way

back to the Tower to settle his business and see his wife
safely away, when a fellow-warder ran into him.

'Off with you, as fast as you can make it,' he said.
'Your prisoners have escaped from the small tower. The
Lieutenant is searching the place for you. If he catches
you, God help you.'

Shaking all over the man rushed back to the messenger. He begged him for the love of God to take him to
the place where the horses were waiting. The messenger
took him and found Richard Fulwood waiting with two
horses.

He rode off and Richard took him to the house of one
of my friends about a hundred miles from London.

When the Lieutenant discovered that his prisoners and
their warder had made off, he went to the Council, taking
with him the letters I had left behind. The Lords of
Council were amazed at the way I had escaped. One of
them, a leading Councillor, said to a gentleman in
attendance (as I was told afterwards) that he was glad I
had got away. The Lieutenant asked for authorisation to
search the whole of London and any place suspected but
the others told him it would be no use.*

'You can't hope to find him,' they said. 'If he has
friends who are prepared to do all this for him, you can
count on it, they will have no difficulty in finding him

---

* '*1597, Oct. 5 – This night there are escaped two prisoners out of the
Tower, viz. John Arden and John Garret. Their escape was made very little
before day, for on going to Arden's chamber in the morning I found the ink in
his pen very fresh. The manner of their escape was thus. The gaoler, one
Bonner, conveyed Garret into Arden's chamber when he brought up the keys,
and out of Arden's chamber by a long rope tied over the ditch to a post they
slid down upon the Tower wharf. This Bennet is also gone this morning at the
opening of the gates . . . I have sent hue and cry to Gravesend, and to the
Mayor of London for a search to be made in London and in all the liberties.*'
Sir John Peyton, Lieutenant of the Tower of London to the Privy Council.
Hat. Cal., vii, pp. 417–18. [*sic; original spellings of names retained.*]

horses and a hiding-place and keeping him well out of your reach.'

A search was made in one or two places. As far as I could discover, nobody of note was taken.

In 1606, following the Gunpowder Plot (in which he was implicated), Gerard fled abroad in disguise. He died in Rome in 1637.

2

The Attempted Escape of Charles I,
King of England,
from Carisbrooke Castle in the Isle of Wight,
Monday, 20th March, 1648

'I could do nothing but sigh and weep for two nights and a day,'
wrote the Royalist Sir John Oglander, when he heard that
Charles I had entered, under escort, into Carisbrooke Castle, in
the November of 1647. 'And the reason of my grief was that I
verily believed he could not come into a worse place for himself,
and where he could be more securely kept.' By the beginning of
the following year, 1648, the King was firmly held prisoner in
the Castle. His household was purged of sympathisers early in
February, and among those dismissed was the laundress, Mrs
Wheeler, and her assistant, Mistress Mary, who had smuggled
letters to and from the King.

The King had lost not only a courier but an efficient
laundry service. Although a replacement was arranged
for the laundress, Mrs Wheeler, the King later complained to Sir Philip Warwick: 'Whilst I have been here
among them I have wanted linen.' A Royalist news-
letter complained at the end of March that Hammond
'was moved that the King might have a Laundresse for
his Lynnen, to which he replied, he could prevent his
fowling so much linnen by debarring His walking, and
that he (himself) wore but two shirts a week, and he

33

thought they were enough for any honest Man.'

The dismissal of some of the servants had still not cleared the castle of Royalist agents. Two in particular were active at this time. The first was Abraham Dowcett, clerk of the kitchen. Born at Rouen, where his uncle was governor, he was brought up a Protestant, and was in King Charles's service as early as 1629, when he served abroad under the Earl of Holland. On his return he had been made Page of the Bedchamber, and he was evidently trusted enough by Parliament to be allowed into his present post at Carisbrooke. Dowcett's job was mainly to help the sub-laundress Mary in getting letters to and from the King.

He seems to have been of a nervous temperament and hardly suited to secret work, for the King, found it necessary to encourage him from time to time. 'Be confident th^t I will be as carefull as you cane be, for y^r discovery will prejudice me as much as You, nor will I needlesly employ you in this Kynde,' he wrote on 13th January. 'Let not Cautiousnesse begett feare,' he added on 19th January, '& be confident of me.'

The letters to Dowcett were in plain language, with personal names represented by code letters. The method of transmission was simple enough. It was part of Dowcett's job to be in attendance when the King took a meal. If there were letters to collect, Charles would make some small sign at the table, and Dowcett would take the first chance of picking them up from the bedroom, whether or not the King was there. 'I shall not blame you,' Charles wrote in one of his later letters, 'though you hazard not to fetch this, untill I be gone to Bowles: which is at that hower every day as I conceave you may come in heither without much danger.' For communication at the meal table the King arranged various signs. 'Y^r right hand bare, for th^e receipt of this, then if th^e last Packett you had from me: which indeed

was of importance & haste: went awaye upon Munday:
let fall y^r hankercher: if since: let fall one of your gloves:
besydes when you have given this Packett to B: [*Mistress
Mary*] tell me newes of fresh Sparagos from London: &
if she tells you that she believes she will be able to ob-
serve my directions: then tell my newes of Artichockes.'
As a further precaution the King's manner to Dowcett
was curt. 'You must not take it ill that I looke sowerly
upon you in publick.'

If Dowcett was at best a reluctant messenger, the
King at least had an active agent in Henry Firebrace, a
Page of the Bedchamber. Firebrace, now twenty-eight
years old, had been for some years in the service of
Parliament, having been secretary to the Earl of Denbigh.
Given a job as servant to the King at Newcastle early in
1647, he had soon been converted to the Royalist cause,
but remained unsuspected by Parliament. When many
of the royal servants eventually followed the King from
Hampton Court to the Isle of Wight, Firebrace went
with them, taking such oddly assorted documents as an
official pass from the Speaker of the House of Commons
and letters from various Royalist contacts in London.
Once in Carisbrooke Castle he immediately sensed the
changed atmosphere. The degree of watchfulness around
the King was such that the safe delivery of his bundle of
letters taxed even Firebrace's ingenuity. As Page of the
Bedchamber he had access to the King's bedroom during
the day while it was empty. He took the chance to hide
his letters there in 'a very convenient and private place'.
That night, as the King was preparing for bed, Firebrace
was able to slip him a note telling him where the papers
were hidden. As soon as the King had gone to prayers
the next morning Firebrace looked in the same place and
found a reply from the King, approving of the idea and
instructing Firebrace to continue using the same hiding
place for his correspondence. It was to serve for several

weeks, supplied by two couriers employed by Firebrace.

With the tightening of security in January, and the appointment of four conservators, Firebrace managed to turn this development to his advantage. Two conservators were always in attendance. During the day, when the King was in his room, they would wait on guard outside each of the two doors. After the King had retired for the night they would sleep outside the door, with their beds right up against the door so that it would not open without the beds being moved. The household servants took their supper after the King had retired, and one night Firebrace approached one of the conservators and offered to take over his duty while he went for some supper. The offer was gratefully accepted, and Firebrace was left with free access to the backstairs door of the King's room, at its south-east corner. It was now possible, through the partly opened door, to carry on a muted conversation with the King without being overheard by the guard on the far side. The King was delighted, and told Firebrace to make this arrangement as often as he could. From now on, there were many evenings when Hammond's trusted conservator could be found stuffing himself with supper downstairs, while conspiratorial whispers were exchanged through the backstairs door.

This arrangement carried one obvious risk. If anyone approached, it was necessary to shut the door and then slide the conservat‵r's bed back up against it, and this took time. Firebrace accordingly thought of an improvement. The walls were covered with tapestry hangings, and under cover of these he pierced a small hole through the wall. This chink, they found, served just as well as the open door, and if anyone was heard approaching, they had only to let the tapestry fall back into place.

In this way Firebrace was able to pass on all the news that filtered into the castle, and to discuss possible ways of escape. The idea finally adopted was that of an escape through the bedroom window, at night with the help of three other people: John Newland, a burgess and merchant of Newport, who had a ship at his disposal, and who could apparently be relied on as a Royalist sympathiser; Edward Worsley, the twenty-seven-year-old son of John and Cecily Worsley of Gatcombe, about one-and-a-half miles south of Carisbrooke, who throughout the war had been identified with the local Royalists; and Richard Osborne, described by Clarendon as 'by extraction a Gentleman', who was now one of the servants at Carisbrooke. Having been recommended by his patron Lord Wharton, and being regarded as loyal to Parliament, Osborne was given the job of Gentleman Usher in daily waiting on the King. One of his jobs was to hold the King's gloves during meals, and he took the chance of slipping into one of the fingers a note offering his help to the King. Charles scented a trap, and suspected this unknown servant of being a Parliamentary agent; but Osborne was soon accepted as one of the inner circle of conspirators, and the King's reliance on him proved justified.

The germ of the new plan was the fact, noticed by Firebrace, that the inner courtyard of the castle did not seem to be patrolled at night, so there was little chance of interference while the King was climbing out of his window. He was to lower himself down to the courtyard with a rope previously provided by Firebrace, and the two of them would then cross the courtyard and go up to the battlements on the curtain wall, presumably on the south side which was remote from the officers' quarters against the north curtain and the gatehouse and guard rooms on the west. Here Firebrace was to pay out a longer rope with a stick fastened across the end for the King to sit on, so that he could be lowered down to the top of the bank at the base of the curtain wall – a drop of fifteen feet. Negotiating on his own the scramble down the bank and into the sunken 'covered way', the King would find as his last obstacle the Elizabethan fortifications beyond the curtain wall. The drop here was only nine feet, and he would be helped down by Osborne and Worsley, who would be waiting there with a spare horse ready saddled, and pistols and riding boots for the King when he came over the wall. Waiting on the coast 'in a convenient place' was John Newland, with 'a lusty Boat' ready to take the King to whichever port he chose. The scheme was worked out in detail and every stage of it carefully checked.

'Every one,' wrote Firebrace, 'was well instructed in his part.' The King, who had lately been keeping to his room, was suddenly seen walking round the castle again, sometimes two or three times a day. He was actually surveying the escape route. As he went, apparently aimlessly, round the battlements, he was being shown the point on the curtain wall at which he was to be let down by Firebrace, and also the position where he had to get over the outer wall. The King himself was confident. To one of his few correspondents in the secret he wrote that the plan had 'great probability of success'. Firebrace's optimism was qualified only by doubts about the principal actor. 'Soe well have I order'd the business,' he wrote on 7th March to the Earl of Lanark, 'as nothing but (himselfe can lett) [*hinder*] it.'

All the arrangements were now complete, and the night of Monday, 20th March, was settled for the attempt. Unobtrusively the escape boat came on station, and as darkness closed over the castle Osborne and Worsley cautiously approached the outer wall with their three horses. One by one the candles went out in the various apartments of the castle, and Firebrace came into the courtyard, his ears straining for any unexpected movement of one of the night sentries. The convivial sounds coming from the guard rooms in the gatehouse had alcoholic overtones that Firebrace found reassuring. As his eyes became accustomed to the starlight he looked up at the two small windows of the King's bedroom, thirteen feet above the courtyard. The light there, like all the others, had now gone out, but he knew that the prisoner was there at the window, ears alert for a signal from outside. The rope for the first stage of the escape had been safely smuggled into the room. The elaborate plan was about to begin.

With a final look round to make sure the courtyard was empty, Firebrace approached the King's window and sent a small stone tinkling up against the glass. He held his breath as he heard the window being furtively opened, followed by a scuffling noise as the King began to squeeze out. Occasional gasps indicated the effort that was being expended. Then Firebrace heard the King groaning, and at this point all his optimism drained away. He knew too well what had happened.

Firebrace and the King had already had some argument about the width of the opening in the barred window, Firebrace maintaining that it would be necessary to remove the bar. The King replied that he had tried, one night, fitting his head through, and he considered the opening was wide enough. Firebrace, still unconvinced, proposed widening the opening a little 'by cutting the plate the Casement shut to at the bottome: wch then might have been easily put by.' He probably meant by this, cutting through the seating of the base of the bar and then bending it aside. The King replied, with some justification, that previous tampering of this sort would mean running the risk of discovery. He told Firebrace to get on with all the other arrangements, and leave him to worry about the window, which he was sure he could negotiate.

This miscalculation proved fatal to the carefully laid escape, and it was no satisfaction to Firebrace, fretting impotently down in the courtyard, to be thus proved right. By now, if he was interpreting correctly the sounds from above, the King was tightly wedged in the window, unable to move in either direction. Firebrace peered up anxiously in an effort to pierce the darkness, his mind racing with possible ways of meeting the crisis. Then he saw something that at least partly reassured him. A candle had been lit and placed in the window, as a signal that the King had got back inside and abandoned the escape. The mortifying sound of distant laughter from the guard rooms served only to emphasise how nearly the King had come to taking his jailers by surprise.

Firebrace morosely made his way to the appointed place on the castle wall. Somewhere in the darkness beyond it, his two fellow-conspirators were keeping their bleak and hazardous rendezvous. He had to get them away before some chance patrol stumbled across them. To hail them at forty yards' distance from the curtain wall would probably have penetrated even the fuddled hearing of the guards; but he still had his handful of stones and he proceeded to throw these, one by one, at the spot where his friends were waiting. Presently he knew from the subdued jingle of harness that they were moving away. The plan had collapsed in ruins, but he had at least performed his last duty for that night: he had brushed over the trail. Now at last he could go to bed.

Abraham Dowcett later fled abroad, joining Charles II's court in Holland. Firebrace and Worsley both lived to see the restoration of the young king, in 1660, and to enjoy their reward for the service they had done his father: Firebrace was made Clerk of the Kitchen, dying peacefully in 1691, and Edward Worsley was knighted by Charles II at Carisbrooke in 1665 and lived out the century, dying in 1702 at the age of eighty-one.

Charles I was executed in Whitehall on 30th January, 1649, less than a year after his attempted escape from Carisbrooke.

3

The Escape of Henry Pitman, surgeon, from a slave plantation in Barbados, having been transported there in 1685 after the Monmouth Rebellion, 9th May, 1687

As a necessary introduction to the following *Relation*, it will be convenient that I give account of the Occasion of my being engaged with the rest that went in to the Duke of Monmouth;* and how far I was concerned in that action.

Being, at that time, but newly returned from a voyage to Italy, I went to see my relations at Sandford in Somersetshire: where I had not been long, before the Duke landed at Lyme; and making forwards, was advanced as far as Ilminster. Upon which, I was induced (partly out of my own curiosity, and partly by the importunity of some of my acquaintance) to go and see whether his strength and number were answerable to what the common rumour had spread abroad: and to that purpose, rode, accompanied by my brother and some other friends, to Taunton; whither the Duke by this

* *James Scott, Duke of Monmouth, eldest illegitimate son of Charles II of England: on 11th June, 1685, four months after Charles II's death, he landed at Lyme Regis in Dorset to raise a rebellion against the new king, his uncle, the Catholic James II.*

time was marching, with such forces as he had got together.

After some stay there, having fully satisfied my curiosity, by a full view both of his person and his army; I resolved to return home: and in order thereunto, I took the direct road back again, with a friend, who had the same intention as myself: but understanding, upon the road, that if we went forward, we should be certainly intercepted by the Lord of Oxford's Troop, then in our way; we found ourselves, of necessity, obliged to retire back again to the Duke's forces, till we could meet with a more safe and convenient opportunity.

But, after some time, losing my horse, and no opportunity presenting itself, I was prevailed with, by the importunate desires of my friends and acquaintance then in the army, to stay and take care of the sick and wounded men. To which I was the rather induced, in regard I thought myself liable to the same punishment, should the Duke be defeated, as those who still remained in the army: but more especially, for that I saw many sick and wounded men miserably lamenting the want of chirurgeons to dress their wounds. So that pity and compassion on my fellow creatures, more especially being my brethren in Christianity, obliged me to stay and perform the duty of my calling among them, and to assist my brother chirurgeons towards the relief of those that, otherwise, must have languished in misery; though, indeed, there were many who did, notwithstanding our utmost care and diligence. Whose lives, perhaps, might have been preserved to this day, had we had a garrison wherein to have given them rest; and not have been constrained, through the cruelty and inhumanity of the King's soldiers, to expose their wounded and fractured limbs to the violent agitation and shogging of the carts, in our daily marches.

But as I was never in arms myself, so neither was I

wanting in my care to dress the wounds of many of the
King's soldiers, who were prisoners in the Duke's army:
using the utmost of my care and skill for both. And thus
I continued in full employment, dressing the wounded
in the night-time and marching by day: till the fatal
rout and overthrow of the whole army [*at Sedgmoor on
6th July, 1685*].

*Captured in his flight homewards, Pitman was tried at Wells
Assizes before Judge Jeffreys.*

Notwithstanding his large promises of grace and
favour, we were all condemned 'to be hanged, drawn,
and quartered'. And by his order, there were two hundred and thirty executed; besides a great number hanged
immediately after the Fight.

The rest of us were ordered to be transported to the
Caribbee Islands. And in order thereunto, my brother
and I, with nearly a hundred more, were given to
Jeremiah Nepho: and by him, sold to George Penne, a
needy Papist.

And in order to our transportation, we were removed
to Weymouth, and shipped on board a vessel that belonged to London: which, in a few days, sailed for Barbadoes, where we arrived in about five weeks' time; but
had a very sickly passage, insomuch that nine of my
companions were buried in the sea.

[*In Barbados*] Our diet was very mean. 5 lb of salt Irish
beef, or salt fish, a week, for each man; and Indian or
Guinea Corn [*maize*] ground on a stone, and made into
dumplings instead of bread.

Which coarse and mean fare brought me to a violent
flux [*diarrhoea*], insomuch that I was forced to complain
to my Master, desiring him to allow me some flour, instead of Indian corn, to make dumplings withal; and

humbly recommended to his consideration my Profession and practice, which I hoped would render me deserving of better accommodation than was usually allowed to other Servants.

But he, not moved with pity, angrily replied, 'I should not have so good!'

Whose unkind answer moved me so, that I had the confidence to tell him that 'I would no longer serve him, nor any other, as a Surgeon, unless I were entertained according to the just merits of my Profession and practice; and that I would choose rather to work in the field with the Negroes than to dishonour my Profession by serving him as Physician and Surgeon, and to accept the same entertainment as common Servants.'

My angry Master, at this, was greatly enraged, and the fiery zeal of his immoderate passion was so heightened by some lying stories of a fellow Servant, that he could not content himself with the bare execution of his cane upon my head, arms, and back, although he played so long thereon, like a furious fencer, until he had split it in pieces; but he also confined me close prisoner in the Stocks (which stood in an open place), exposed to the scorching heat of the sun; where I remained about twelve hours, until my Mistress, moved either with pity or shame, gave order for my release.

It would be too tedious to give a particular account of the many other abuses and unkindnesses we received at his hands; and therefore it shall suffice to say, that in this condition we lived with him about fifteen months [*to about April, 1687*], until by his debauched and extravagant course of life, he had run himself so extremely in debt, and particularly to those merchants that sold us to him, that he could not well pay for us. For which reason, we were removed from him; but the merchants were forced to remit the money due for our service, before he would return us.

And now, being returned again, we remained in the merchants' hands, as goods unsold; and because I would not consent to be disposed of, at their pleasure; they threatened to horsewhip me and put me to servile employment.

But we had not been long here, before my brother died, and I being wearied with long and fruitless expectation of my Pardon; and no less perplexed and tired with the great abuses I had received at their hands, resolved to attempt the making of my escape from off the island: to which purpose, after several contrivances and ways that came into my head, and those well weighed with the consequent circumstances that possibly I could foresee; I concluded at length to proceed after this manner.

Being introduced by a friend into the acquaintance of one John Nuthall [*a debtor*] a carver; whose condition was somewhat mean, and therefore one that wanted money to carry him off the island: I imparted my design unto him, and employed him to buy a boat of a Guiney Man [*a ship trading to Guinea*] that lay in the road; promising him for his reward, not only his passage free, and money for his present expenses, but to give him the boat also, when we arrived at our port.

By the way, it is to be understood, that the means which enabled me to defray these extraordinary expenses, was a private consignation of goods from my relations, to a particular friend in the island; who took care to dispose of them for me.

John Nuthall therefore readily consented to what I proposed; and after I had enjoined him to secrecy, I delivered him £12 to buy the boat; which accordingly he did, and gave in security for the same at the Secretary's Office, conformable to the custom and laws of the island. Nevertheless all that would not prevent the jealousy of the magistrates, that sprang from the consideration of his poverty, and the little service they knew the boat would do him.

Whereupon, they sent for John Nuthall, and strictly commanded him to discover who it was that had employed him to buy the boat; and threatened to put him to his oath. Nevertheless, they could get nothing out of him, for the man had so much courage that he confidently denied that any person had employed him; but that he bought the boat merely for his own use. Yet was not all this sufficient. They still threatened to seize the boat, unless he gave in better security. Upon which, he came to me, to advise what it were best to be done. I ordered him forthwith to sink the boat: which as it very much abated the suspicion of the Magistrates, so it secured the boat from seizure.

In this interval of time, the boat being sunk, and by that means, the suspicion of the Magistrates quite over; we began to think of providing necessaries for our intended voyage; which as they occurred to my thoughts, I set them down, that so nothing might be forgotten. Which take as followeth. A hundredweight of bread, a convenient quantity of cheese, a cask of water, some few bottles of Canary and Maderia wine and beer; these being for the support of Nature: and then for use, a compass, quadrant, chart, half-hour glass, half-minute glass, log and line, large tarpaulin, a hatchet, hammer, saw and nails, some spare boards, a lantern and candles. All which were privately conveyed to a friend's house, not far from the water side, to be in a readiness against the time.

Which after I had bethought myself; who besides, to make choice of for my companions was the next thing to be considered of; but that a lucky chance, after a short expectation, presented itself to us.

For within few days the Governor of Mevis putting in at the Barbadoes; the Governor, for his more noble entertainment, caused the Militia of the town to be in arms: which was attended with revelling, drinking, and feasting to excess; the consequence of which, I easily conjectured would be drowsy security and carelessness.

This time, I therefore thought most proper for our intended enterprise; and gave notice thereof to my intended companions (most of whom I kept ignorant of my design until now, fearing it should by any means be discovered): and ordered them not to carry home their arms, but to bring them, after it was night, to a certain storehouse by the wharf; where I designed to put to sea. The storehouse was then under the care of John Whicker, one of my confederates; and therefore a most happy convenience to conceal both them and their arms, till it was time to sail.

In the meantime, John Nuthall employed two lusty blacks to empty the water out of our skiff, and set her afloat; and then brought her to the wharf before the storehouse: whither by this time, we had conveyed our necessaries; keeping the blacks within the storehouse, that they might have no opportunity to discover our design.

About 11 o'clock at night [*9th May, 1687*], thinking it time to embark in our small vessel, we assigned one of our company to stand sentry at the head of the wharf, to give us notice if the Watch should happen to come that way; and then, with all speed, we put our provisions and necessaries aboard: which we had no sooner done, but we had an alarm that the Watch was approaching to the head of the wharf. A misfortune which so surprised us, that we all, of an instant, betook ourselves to our heels. And I, for my own part, soon recovered a friend's house, giving all for lost; supposing my companions were fallen into the enemy's hands.

But whilst I was condoling my misfortune to my friend, and giving him a lamentable account of our attempt and discovery; and also consulting whether to retire in the country, to lie dormant if possible till some better opportunity offered itself, I heard a person at the window inquiring for me.

At first, I was in a dreadful fear, lest it was one of the Watch in quick pursuit after me: but knowing him, by his voice to be one of my companions, I gladly received the account he gave me. Which was, that the Watch came only to call up one of their number, that was to watch with them that night; and then went away, without taking the least notice of the boat.

However, I was so disheartened by this unlucky accident, that I was altogether unwilling to make a second attempt, till at length overruled by the importunity of my friend; more especially when he told me that they all waited for me, and could not go without me, for none of them had any skill in navigation. So, considering the baseness of disappointing so many persons, whom I had engaged in so much danger; I resolved, once more, to hazard a burnt forehead and sore back: and going with him to the water side, I found my companions by the boat, waiting for me, and not a little glad to see me come again.

We embarked in our small vessel; being in number eight, viz., John Wicker, Peter Bagwell, William Woodcock, John Cooke, Jeremiah Atkins, and myself, which were Sufferers on the account of the Duke of Monmouth: the other two were John Nuthall, who bought the boat for me, and Thomas Walker. Thomas Austin was so possessed with fear of being cast away, that he would not go with us.

About midnight, we put off to sea, designing for Curaçoa, a Dutch island that lies about 200 leagues thence: for we durst not go to any English island, for fear we should be taken and sent back.

We rowed softly forward, within a pistol's shot of the

Fort; and there lay at that time, a man-of-war in the road: which made us not a little afraid of being discovered by those watchful enemies; but Providence so ordered it, that we passed both without discovery.

However, by the time that we were got clear of the Fort and the shipping, our boat being so extremely leaky, had taken in so much water that we were almost ready to sink; not daring to heave it out before, for fear of making a noise to alarm our enemies.

But having the conveniency of a tub and a large wooden bowl; we now fell to work, and in a little time, we pretty well emptied our boat: and then we set our mast, and hoisted our sail, and steered our course southwest as near as I could judge, intending to make the Great Grenada. Our candles being bruised into one mass of tallow, and our tinder and matches being wet, we could not strike a light to steer by our compass; neither indeed had we any candles lighted for the same reason, during our whole voyage: so that, in the night, we were forced to steer by the stars; and when it was cloudy, by the wind.

That which troubled us most was the leakiness of our little vessel. For although we endeavoured all we could to stop her gaping seams with our linen and all the rags we had, which we tallowed with our bruised candles: yet she was so thin, so feeble, so heavily ladened, and wrought so exceedingly by reason of the great motion of the sea, that we could not possibly make her tight, but were forced to keep one person almost continually, day and night, to throw out the water, during our whole voyage.

The same night, most of my companions were so seasick, that notwithstanding we were all ready to sink, I could hard persuade them to throw out the water; and my place being at the helm, to guide and govern the boat, I could not safely go thence. However, at length, through great importunity and earnest persuasions, I prevailed with them to take a little pain to preserve us from drowning. My companions now began to wish themselves at Barbadoes again; and would willingly have returned: but I told them there was no possibility of it, being so far to the leeward of the island.

One of them, through carelessness in heaving out the water, threw over our wooden bowl; and we running away with a large wind, could not go back to take it up; so that we had nothing left to throw out the water with, but our tub; which obliged them to be more careful of it, for our lives were concerned therein.

May the 10th [*1687*], in the morning, we were got almost out of sight of the island; at least far enough from being descried from thence. And perceiving no sort of vessel in pursuit of us, we began to be cheered up with the thoughts of our liberty, and the hopes of our safe arrival at our desired port.

But then, alas, the night no sooner approached, but we were assailed with a brisk gale of wind; under which misfortune, another worse befel us, that we split our rudder so that we were forced to lower our sail, and with an oar to keep our boat before the sea, whilst one of my company, a joiner, mended our helm by nailing to it two pieces of boards. That done, we went cheerily on again.

May the 11th, we had indifferent good weather. My companions being pretty well recovered of their sea-sickness, we now had time to put things in a better posture in our boat; and to raise her, which we did by nailing on tarpolings from her sides to our oars that were lashed fast about nine inches above, which did us good service in keeping out the sea. We likewise made a tilt [*awning*] with a hammock over the hinder part of our boat, to defend us from the scorching heat of the sun.

May the 12th. This morning, notwithstanding we

steered south-west, to weather the Great Grenada, the current had set us so much to the northward, that we made the Grenadilloes to bear west of us: which obliged us to steer more southerly to weather the Great Grenada.

May the 13th. The last night, we weathered the Great Grenada, and steered down the south side of the same; and then shaped our course for the Testigos. For I could not take any true observation by my quadrant, because of the uneven motion of the sea, and the nearness of the sun to the zenith, and therefore was constrained to steer a course from island to island, though the further way about.

May the 14th. We had fair weather, and a fresh gale of wind; and about noon, as I remember, we made the Testigos, bearing south-south-west; and before night, made the north-east end of the Margarita.

But, by this time, being so extremely spent for want of sleep, having been obliged for the most part, night and day, to steer the boat; I was desirous to take a little rest: but first I directed one of my companions how to steer down by the said island; and then composed myself to sleep.

In which interval of time, my companions eagerly longing for fresh water, in regard ours stank so extremely as it did, stood in for the land; and lowered the sail, designing to go ashore. At which time, I happily [*by chance*] awoke; and apprehending the great danger of falling into the hands of the Indians, who had already kindled a fire on the shore not far from us, I caused the sail again to be hoisted up, and hasted away with all expedition: and being favoured with a brisk gale of wind, we soon got out of fear or danger of those savage cannibals.

May the 15th. We had fair weather, and very pleasant sailing down the north side of this island [*Margarita*]. From the west end of this island, we directed our course for Saltatudos; but that afternoon, the wind increased, and a white ring encircled the moon, which I thought presaged ill weather, and to our great sorrow, proved too true. For about nine at night, a dreadful storm arose, which made us despair of ever seeing the morning sun. And now the sea began to foam, and to turn its smooth surface into mountains and vales. Our boat was tossed and tumbled from one side to the other; and so violently driven and hurried away by the fury of the wind and sea, that I was afraid we should be driven by the island in the night-time: and therefore we brought our boat to, with her head against the sea: but the wind and sea still increasing, we were forced to bear up before it, with only sail sufficient to give her steerage way.

And now, in vain we began to wish ourselves at the Barbadoes again. But the Omnipotent (who is never unmindful of the cries of his people in distress) heard our prayers; so that when all our hopes were given over, and we had resigned ourselves into his hands, expecting every moment when the wide gaping sea would devour and swallow us up: GOD, of his infinite mercy and unspeakable goodness, commanded the violence of the winds to cease, and allayed the fury of the raging waves. Eternal praises to his Name for evermore!

May the 16th. This morning, at break of day, we saw the island of Saltatudos just before us, and when it was sufficiently light, that we could discern how the land lay, we steered down the north side of it, intending to go ashore at some convenient place to refresh ourselves after that dreadful storm, and to take on board some fresh water, and if possible to stop the leaks of our boat, in order to proceed in our voyage for Curaçoa: and accordingly, when we came to the leeward of a small island hard by the other, we stood in directly for the shore, thinking it a convenient place to land. Which we had no sooner done, but we saw a canoe coming thence, directing her course towards us. At which sight, being a little surprised, my companions provided their arms, and charged their muskets and blunderbusses with glass bottles: for we coming from Barbadoes in so great a hurry and fear; through forgetfulness they left their bag of bullets on the wharf.

When they were come somewhat nearer, that we could perceive them to paddle like Indians, we bore up and were running from them.

Which as soon as they perceived, they waved their hats and hailed us; by which we knew they were not Indians as we supposed: and therefore we permitted them to come nearer, and perceiving them to be white men, we enquired 'What they were?'

They told us, 'They were Englishmen in distress, &c., and waited for an opportunity to go off the island.'

The account we gave them of ourselves was very short. That we came from one of the Windward islands: by which, they supposed we had fled for debt; and should have continued in that belief, had not Thomas Walker, one of my companions, privately informed them, That there were only he and John Nuthall that were debtors: the rest of us being rebels: for he thought thereby to ingratiate himself and friend in their friendship.

But these privateers, for so they were, as we afterwards understood, hated them the more for their treachery; and loved us the better, confessing that they were rebels too, adding that 'if the Duke of Monmouth had had 1000 of them, they would soon have put to flight the King's army.'

After we had sufficiently refreshed ourselves with rest and sleep, and returned to the LORD the praises due to his Name, for his wonderful and miraculous deliverance; we thought it time to consider how to stop the leaks of our boat, and to raise a deck over her with rinds [*barks*] of trees, &c., that we might proceed in our intended voyage for Curaçoa.

Our intentions were no sooner perceived by the privateers, but they endeavoured to persuade us from it: alleging the insufficiency of our boat, and the dangers we were so lately exposed unto; and advising us rather to go with them in their pereagoes [*piraguas*] a-privateering than to hazard our lives by a second attempt. With the like argument, they would have easily prevailed with my companions to consent to go with them; had I not persuaded them to the contrary.

But when the privateers saw it was in vain to persuade, they thought to compel us, by burning our boat: supposing then that we would choose rather to go with them, than to stay upon the island till shipping came for salt, which would be eight or nine months; and in the meantime, to be in danger of being taken by the Spaniards for privateers, or otherwise to be starved with hunger, for we had no more than 4lb or 5lb of bread for each man left.

But this contrivance answered not their expectations. For notwithstanding they burnt our boat and took our sails and other utensils from us, I continued my resolution, and chose rather to trust Divine Providence on that desolate and uninhabitable island than to partake or be any ways concerned with them in their piracy: having confidence in myself, that GOD, who had so wonderfully and miraculously preserved us on the sea and brought us to this island, would, in like manner, deliver us hence, if we continued faithful to Him.

About the 25th of May, 22 of the privateers, having first raised the sides of their pereagoes with boards, fastened with the nails they saved in the burning of our boat, and fitted them for sea; they set sail: leaving four of their company behind, that refused to go with them; as also a Spanish boat that was of no service to them, neither could be of any use to us, unless we had sails to sail her, and a rudder to guide her, both of which we wanted.

In this situation, they left us, deprived of all ways and means of getting off until the season aforesaid: unless GOD, by a particular Providence, should direct some vessel or other to touch here.

Pitman and his companions were abandoned on Tortuga on 25th May, 1687. For the next three months they lived on turtles and fish. They salted and dried fish ready for the winter, built themselves small thatched cabins, stitched their clothes with bone needles and dried leaf-vein 'thread', and in general, settled down to make the best of it. In August a second privateering ship appeared off-shore. Its crew had heard of Pitman and his companions from the pirates who had abandoned them on the island in May. They invited Pitman aboard and received him honourably, 'the trumpets in the meantime sounding', and agreed to take him as a passenger. They would not, however, take his companions, though they did provide stores for them.

Pitman accordingly set sail with the privateers. Hearing from the crew of a trading ketch, with which they fell in company on the sea, that a small new settlement had been set up eight months before at Providence in the Bahamas, they sailed there, to find a thriving, hopeful, democratic community, under a sober elected governor who preached to the people on the first day of every week. The privateers beached their ship at Providence, gave their guns to the settlers to defend the island, burned the ship, divided their goods, and split up to 'betake themselves to an honest course of life'. Pitman transferred into the trading ketch and sailed with her to New York, where he had the pleasure of encountering an acquaintance from Barbados and hearing of the rage which had greeted his escape, the punishments planned for him, and the belief that he and his company must have perished at sea. He then took passage under a false name for Amsterdam, and when the ship put into Cowes in the Isle of Wight, quitted her and went ashore. 'I returned in a disguise to my relations, who before this time, unknown to me, had procured my Pardon; and joyfully received me as one risen from the dead.'

Of Pitman's companions, Nuthall and Walker fitted out the rudderless Spanish boat and tried to escape from Tortuga; but the boat was 'large and unruly', their navigational skill was non-existent, and they were never heard of again. The others seized yet another ex-privateering boat, set sail, were captured by the Spaniards, and were used as slave labour aboard ship. Atkins died and was tossed overboard, but the rest survived, were eventually ransomed, and got home at last.

4

The Escape of William Maxwell, 5th Earl of Nithsdale, imprisoned in the Tower of London in 1715 following the Jacobite Rising, Friday, 23rd February, 1716

Lord Nithsdale was captured at the battle of Preston and sent to the Tower of London. He was sentenced to be executed on 24th February. The following account is taken from a letter written, some time later, by his wife Winifred Countess of Nithsdale, to her sister, Lady Lucy Herbert, who was the Abbess of the English Augustine Nuns at Bruges in Belgium. In it, her description of her appeal to George I, which she placed at the end of her account, has been transposed to its proper place in the sequence of events. On 22nd February, two days before the date fixed for his execution, Lord Nithsdale wrote a letter of farewell to his brother and sister, commending his wife and children to their care. 'You have been informed by my orders of what has passed here relating to me,' he wrote, 'and what my dearest wife has done for me, so all I shall say is, that there cannot be enough said in her praise. Everybody admires her, everybody applauds her, and extols her for the proofs she has given me of her love.' Next day she was to show still greater proof of her love and resolution.

Dear Sister,

My Lord's escape is such an old story now, that I have almost forgot it, but since you desire the account, to whom I have too many obligations to refuse anything that is in my power, I will endeavour to call it to mind, and be as exact in the relation as I can possible.

I think I owe myself the justice to begin by the motives I had to attempt so hazardous an enterprise, which I fully intended not to go about till the very last, foreseeing all the difficulties, which could not be surmounted without a particular protection of almighty God, but rely'ed it would not be refused me, when all human resources failed. You must then know, that when I first came to London, which I did as soon as ever I heard of my Lord's being in the Tower, and his earnest desire I should, he, as he sent me word, having nobody to help him till I came, upon which I rode to Newcastle, and took the coach there to York, but there fell so much snow, that when I came thither, the York coach could not go, so I took horses and rode to London. Through such weather, the very post stopped some days, and we were up to the horse girts in snow: however, I got safe and without accident.

When arrived, I went immediately and solicited all the persons in power, without the least hopes given me of any favour; all the contrary, everyone was so plain as to tell me that perhaps some of the prisoners might be pardoned, but not him for certain. I begged to know the occasion of this distinction, but could obtain no answer to that point, but that they would not flatter me, which, though they did not tell me, well did I know the reasons: a Catholic upon the Borders, and one who had a great following, and whose family had ever upon all occasions stuck to the royal family, and the only support the Catholics had, amongst that Whigish part of the country, would be well out of the way. They had not yet forgot that his grandfather held out, as the last garrison in Scotland, his own Castle of Carlaverock, and rendered it up but by the King's own orders, so that, now they had him in their power, they were resolved not to let him slip out of their hands.

My Lord had a great inclination to have a petition given, thinking it might be of benefit; for my part, I did not think it would be of any, but was willing to content him, so desired him to have his petition drawn, and I would find a way to deliver it, notwithstanding all the precaution the Elector* had taken to avoid it; so that the first day I knew he was to go to the drawing room, I dressed myself in a black manteau and petticoat, as if in mourning, and sent to Mrs Morgan, the same as went with me to the Tower afterwards, for I did not know the Elector, and might have taken another for him, and she did, so would show me the right.

I had another gentlewoman with me, but I forgot who, but we went all three into the chamber that was between his closet and the drawing room, so that he was to pass the whole length of the room to go to it, and there being three windows in it, we sat ourselves upon the middle one, that I might have time to catch him before he could get by, which I did, and knelt down and presented my petition, telling him in French that I was the unhappy Countess of Nithsdale, that he might not pretend he knew not who I was, but finding him going without taking my petition, I took hold of the skirt of his coat, that he might stay to hear me; but he endeavoured to get away, and I held so fast that he drew me upon my knees almost from the middle of the chamber to the drawing room door; at last one of the Blue Ribbons that was with him took me round the waist to draw me back, and another drew the skirt of his coat out of my hand,

* *The Jacobites referred to George I merely as 'Elector of Hanover,' holding that he was not the true king of England and Scotland.*

and the petition that I had endeavoured to put in his pocket fell down in the struggle, and I almost swooned with the trouble; however, one of the gentlemen took up the petition, and as I knew it ought to have been given by him to the Lord of the Bedchamber that was in waiting, I had wrote a letter beforehand, and desired he would do me the favour to have a petition read that I had had the honour to give to the King, as I was then forced to term him. It proved to be my Lord Dorset, by good luck for me, it being one Mrs Morgan was very well acquainted with, she went into the drawing room, and delivered the letter to him, which he took very civilly, but could not then read it, for he was at cards with the Prince, but as soon as the game was ended, he did, and acted as I heard, very warmly and kindly in the matter, to which he was induced the more by the Duke of Montrose, who had seen me as he had passed into the room, and was then coming to speak to me, but I made him a sign not to do it, for fear his taking notice of me might have spoiled my design.

They got my petition to be read more than once, without any effect, but served for the discourse there that night, and my being so rudely treated had made a noise, and gave no good reputation to the Duke of Hanover, for several said, what had they brought themselves to, for the Kings of England was never used to refuse a petition from the poorest woman's hand, and to use a person of my quality in such a manner as he had done, was a piece of unheard of brutality.

Upon which I took the resolution to endeavour his [*her husband's*] escape, but confided my intention to nobody but my dear Evans.* But to concert measures, I solicited earnestly to be permitted to see my Lord, but that was refused me, except I would stay in prison with him; that I would not accept, giving for reason that my

* *Her faithful maid.*

health would not agree with such a confinement; but the true one was, that I would then put myself out of the power of doing what I intended to attempt.

But by means of money to the guards I saw him frequently, till the condemnation, after which, we had leave, the last week, to go and take our leaves of them. I had provided all that was necessary for his disguise, by the means of poor Evans, so had nothing to do but persuade him to make use of them, which I had much difficulty to do. However God Almighty helped me in that also when the time came.

It was on a Thursday, 22nd of February, that our general petition to the House of Lords was given, to beg them to intercede to the King (as we were then forced to call him) to pardon the prisoners, having been disappointed the day before of its being delivered, because the Duke of—, I forget which of the bastard Dukes – had promised Lady Darwentwater to give it, and when it came too, he failed, and as she was an English Countess, it was her business. However, we had still the next day before the execution, in which he promised not to fail. But for fear he should, I engaged the Duke of Montrose, so I was sure of its being done by one or the other, and therefore went with a most numerous train of most of the ladies of quality then in town, to solicit their favour as the Lords went into the Parliament House, who all treated me very civilly. But the favour we got was chiefly due to poor Lord Pembroke, who, though he begged me not to come near him, sent me word he would do all that lay in his power; which he performed fully, for it was upon a speech of his that it passed in our favours.

The occasion of the petition was, that they pretended to dispute the King's power of pardoning prisoners the Parliament had accused. But by the forementioned person's speech it was carried that it was, and they granted our petition to them to intercede to him for mercy; but there rose up one of the Lords, and said they would do so, but with this clause, that it should be for such of them that deserved it, and not in general. This took of all my hopes, for I understood that these deserts consisted in informations of all those that were engaged in the business; and well did I know, nor would I have desired, that my Lord should have purchased his life at that rate; however, the grant in general I thought I might make a benefit of for my design, and with this thought, went straight out of the Parliament House to the Tower, and putting on as cheerful a look as I was able, went up, and told the guards at each place where they were, that I came to bring good news about their prisoners, for there was now no fear for them, the petition having passed in their favour, and then pulled out some small thing out of my pocket, and bid them drink the King's health, and the Peers. What I gave them was no great matter, for I was afraid that if I gave them too liberally they might perhaps think I had some design, and I thought giving of them something would put them in good humour against the next day, which was the last before that appointed for the execution.

The morning after I did not go, but in the afternoon, having too many things to put in readiness. When I was ready to go, I sent to Mrs Mills, in whose house I was lodged, and told her that, finding there was now no further room for hope of my Lord's pardon, nor longer time but this night, I was resolved to endeavour his escape; that I had provided all that was requisite for it, and that I hoped she would not refuse to come along with me, to the end that he might pass for her, and begged she would come immediately, because we were full late.

In the meanwhile, I sent to one Mrs Morgan, who then went by the name of Hilton, one my dear Evans had made me acquainted with, who had rendered me a great service. She I also told my intention to, and desired, she being tall and slender, she would put under her own riding hood one I had provided to put upon Mrs Mills, who was to give hers to my Lord, my intention being that when he came out he should pass for her; she was as tall as him, and being with child, would be about the same bigness.

After which we went into the coach, where I never ceased talking, not to give them leisure to think, for they consented immediately to come with me, the surprise having left them no time to reflect of the consequences.

When we arrived, the first I brought in was Mrs Morgan, for I could carry in but one at once, and she brought in the clothes that was to serve Mrs Mills when she had parted with her own; and after I had stripped her of what she had brought in for me, I conducted her out again, begging she would do me the kindness to send me my woman to drease [*dress*] me, for I began to be afraid I should be too late if she did not come immediately, having a petition to give, which, if I were too late, having but this night, I were undone, so dispatched her safe, and partly downstairs, where I took Mrs Mills, who came in with her handkerchief before her eyes, as it was very natural for a person that came to take leave of a friend that was going to die. I made her do it, that he might go out in the same manner; and her eyebrows being a little upon the yellow, and his very thick and black, I had provided paint of that colour to dye his, and a tour of the same coloured hair, and to hide a long beard that had not time to be shaved, white paint to cover it with, and the rest of his face, and red for the cheeks, all which remainder of the provision I left in the Tower when I went out.

The poor guards, who, upon the little I had given them the night before, were in good humour, let me in and out with my people very willingly, and were not so much upon the *qui vive*, because they were persuaded there would be a pardon upon what I had told them the day before.

I made Mrs Mills put off her own riding hood, and put on that I had brought in, which, when she had done, I took her by the hand and went out with her of my Lord's room, saying as I passed through the other (in which there were nine people) with all the seeming concern imaginable, 'Dear Mrs Chathrin, I must beg you to go in all haste and look for my woman, for she certainly does not know what o'clock it is, and has forgot the petition I am to give, which, should I miss, is irreparable, having but this one night; let her make all the haste she can possible, for I shall be upon thorns till she comes.'

So the persons in the room, who were all the guards' wives and daughters, seemed all to be in pain, and the sentinels at the door opened it very speedily, and when I had seen her out I returned back to my Lord, and made an end of putting him in order. I had taken care that Mrs Mills, when she went out, should not go crying as I had made her come in, because my Lord might pass for the gentlewoman that came in so, having her clothes, which when I had finished to put him on, with all my petticoats but one, it grew pretty dark, and I was afraid of the lighting of the candles, so thought it was time to go, so I came out, leading him by the hand, he had his handkerchief before his eyes, and I spoke to him with the greatest concern in the world, lamenting myself bitterly that Evans was so neglectful, that she had ruined me by her long stay – 'So, dear Mrs Betty, run and bring her with you for God's sake; you know my lodgings, if ever you made haste in your life do it now, for I am almost distracted with this disappointment.'

So the guard opened the door very quickly, and I went with him downstairs, still conjuring him to make haste; but as soon as I got him out of the door, I made him pass before, and I followed him, for fear the sentinel had perceived something by his way of walking, but I still continued to beg him to make haste. At the foot of the stairs I found my dear Evans, into whose hands I put him.

I had engaged Mr Mills to expect him in the place before the Tower, to carry him to some sure place in case we succeeded. But he thought it so improbable that we should, that the surprise at the sight made him lose himself so entirely that he was capable of nothing, which my dear Evans perceiving, and having all the presence of mind imaginable, and having friends of her own she could confide [*trust*], she immediately, without telling him anything, for fear it should strick him, carried him to a place of security, or else we had lost our business after it was done: And having left him there, returned to look for Mr Mills, who by this time was come from his surprise and gone home, and had procured a place for him to stay in, which they carried him to.

In the meanwhile, I who had sent him as it were of a message, was obliged to return upstairs and pass the room again to go to my Lord's in the same seeming perplexity for fear of being too late as I went down in, so that all the poor people seemed to compassionate me mightily.

When I got into my Lord's chamber, I spoke as it were to him, and answered as if he had, and imitated his voice as near as I could, and walked up and down the room, as if we had been walking and talking together, till I thought he had time enough to be out of their reach. I then began to think it was fit for me to get out of it also. So I opened the door, and went half out of it, holding the door in my hand, that what I said might be heard by those without, and took a solemn leave of my Lord for that night, saying that I thought some strange thing must have happened to make Evans stay, she that never used to be neglectful in the smallest thing, to make her so in a matter of this consequence. But I found there was

no remedy but going myself; that if the Tower was still
open when I had done, I would see him that night, but
he might be sure that as soon as ever it was in the morning, I would be with him, and hoped to bring him good
news, and then, before I shut the door, I drew in to the
inside a little string that lifted up a wooden latch, so that
when the string was wanting in the outside, the door
could not be opened but by those within, after which I
shut the door with a flap, that it might be surely shut,
and as I passed by I told my Lord's valet de chamber,
who knew nothing of the matter, that he would not have
candles till he called for them, for that he would finish
some prayers first, and so went downstairs.

And there being several hackney coaches waiting in
the place, I got into one and went to my own lodgings,
where I had left poor Mr Makenzy to stay for the petition
that was to have been given in case my project had
failed, for it was not come before I went. So I told him
there was no need of it now, for my Lord was out of the
Tower and their hands, I hoped, but as yet did not know
where.

*Lady Nithsdale went first to leave a message for the Duchess of
Buccleuch; then continued –*

After which I made one of the servants call me a chair,
and bid them to go to the Duchess of Montrose, who had
all along showed a particular concern for me. She had
left word that in case I came, to say that she was not at
home, because she said she could not see me in the
trouble she knew I would be in, but by some mistake they
brought me up, so there was no remedy. So she came to
me, and as my heart was very light, I smiled when she
came into the chamber, and run to her in great joy. She
really started when she saw me, and since owned that
she thought my head was turned with trouble, till I told

her of my good fortune; after which she begged me to put myself in a place of security, for that she knew the Elector was high displeased with me for the petition I had given him that had occasioned his being complained of. I desired they would give me a chair, for I never kept any fear of being tris'd [*traced*].

The Duchess said she would go to Court and see how the news was received, which she did, and told me the Elector stormed terribly when the account came, and said he was betrayed, for he was sure it could not have been done without connivance, and sent two persons to the Tower immediately to see that the others were well guarded, that they might not do the like. Some said it was one, the other another, and nobody was very sure which, but herself.

After I left her, I went to a house which Evans had found for me beforehand, where she had promised to come and give me notice where my Lord was, which she did soon after I was there, and told me that, after she had left him in security, she went to seek out Mr Mills, who by that time was come from his first surprise, and returned to his own house, where she found him, and that he had carried my Lord from the first place where she put him in the meanwhile to a poor woman's house just before the court of guards. She had but one little room up a small pair of stairs, poor little bed, into which we were forced to go immediately for fear they should hear more walking than usual. She left us a bottle of wine and some bread, and Mrs Mills brought us some more the next day in her pocket, but other thing we got not from Thursday evening to Saturday evening, that Mr Mills came when it was dark, and carried my Lord to the Venetian Ambassador's, who knew nothing of the matter. But one of his servants kept him in his own room till Wednesday, he being to go to Dover by the Ambassador's orders, with a coach and six horses, to bring his

brother from thence; whom he expected by that time. He
put my Lord on a livery coat, and went away before day,
and carried him safe to Dover without the least suspicion, where immediately Mr Michel, which is the
name of the Ambassador's servant, took a small vessel
and went over to Calais with my Lord in so few hours
that the master of it said 'If we were flying for our lives
we could not have a fairer wind,' which he said by
chance, little thinking that he had one in it that was in
that case.

This is as full an account as I can give you of that
affair, and of all those concerned in it, and I assure you
is as near as I can possibly remember just as it passed, and
you may depend upon the truth.

For my part, I went into a very honest man's house in
Drury Lane, but whose name I do not remember, and
lay quiet until I heard my Lord was safe on the other
side of the water.

*Although by remaining in the British Isles she put herself in
danger of arrest, Lady Nithsdale rode north again ('though I had
never rid but the fore-mentioned journey from York') to rescue
the family papers which she had buried in the garden; their loss
might have affected her son's inheritance. She then hurried back
to London and 'lay quiet until the hubbub and search was over'.*

In the meanwhile I took the advice of a very honest and
famous lawyer, who was of opinion that it was fit for me
to be gone, after the search for me was over; which
advice I followed about a fortnight after, and got safe
without accident. The reason he gave me for it was, that
though in all other cases a wife could not be pursued for
making her husband's escape, but in matter of treason,
according to the rigour of the law, a wife's head answers
for her husband's, and the Elector was so enraged at me
that they would not answer what might happen; so

begged me to be gone. The reason of this great displeasure had been augmented by a petition I had given him, notwithstanding his orders that nobody should offer to come with any of the prisoners' wives to give him any, for he was resolved not to be troubled with any. [*This*] made the Elector have a particular dislike to me, which he showed afterwards, for when all the ladies whose Lords had been concerned in this business, put in claims for their jointures, mine was given amongst the rest, but he said I was not, nor did deserve the same privilege; so I was excepted, and he would never hear speak in my favour. This made everyone of opinion I was better out of the way, for in the fury they were then against me, it was not advisable for me to venture the falling into their hands; upon which I went off.

This is the full relation of what you desired, and of all the transactions that I passed at that time, which nobody but yourself could have obtained from me, for whom my obligations has imposed me a law of never refusing any that lies in my power. You will excuse all mistakes in this long scroll, for it being only to you, I relied on your goodness in that, and have had no other regard but to the truth, that you may depend on; and all other faults you must excuse.

Lady Nithsdale travelled to Paris where she met her husband and children. They stayed for a short time at the Pretender's Court, but then retired to Rome where they lived peacefully together for many years. Lord Nithsdale died in 1744 and his wife did not long survive him.

5

The Escape of Stewart Carmichael of Bonnyhaugh, imprisoned in the transport 'Pamela' off Tilbury, following the '45 Jacobite Rising, September, 1746

Following the defeat of the Jacobite army at Culloden on 16th April, 1746, the Revd Mr James Taylor, Episcopal minister in Thurso, Caithness, was warned that 'a sort of warrant' had been issued, directing the sheriff to arrest him and to burn his meeting house. He accordingly left his house and lodged with friends, privately, until he received letters from Sir James Stuart of Burray, in the Orkneys, inviting him to go to Burray and promising him 'all the security his interest was able to afford'. Mr Taylor crossed to Flottay on 17th May and reached Burray on the following day, to be warmly welcomed.

About two days thereafter Sir James was informed that Master Moodie of Melsater, then a lieutenant of foot in the British service, had accepted a commission to come north, in company with some ships of war design'd for the Orknays and Western Islands, in order to search for and apprehend his person, and to burn his house, etc. And on Friday the 23rd of said month [*May*] Sir James was again warned by a gentleman of integrity that if Moodie was not already in Orknay, he was certainly hovering near its coast, and earnestly press'd him to provide for his own and ladie's security. The next day, in the forenoon, several ships appear'd and made to Holm Sound, where some of them anchor'd, and others held on their course to Stromness. About eight of the clock at night two or three big ships past by Burray the same way. About ten o'clock Sir James commanded to send a boat to Holm Sound for intelligence, which was detain'd by Mr Moodie; and this might have convinc'd Sir James that it was high time to shift for himself. But neither this nor any other warnings could prevail with him to leave his own house and avoid the impending danger, which proceeded (perhaps) from a consciousness of his innocence, though some people believ'd it to be the effect of another cause. For had he duly considered the unwearied malice which the numerous party that follow'd the Earl of Morton in that country (who had for several years gone all lengths heedless fury was capable to drive them, to blacken his character and ruin his interest) continued still to bear against him, he would have certainly retired to some other country, and remain'd till the heat of the prosecutions had somewhat abated.

Between three and four of the morning on Sunday the 25th [*May*], Mr Taylor was alarm'd in his bedroom by one of the servants, who begg'd him immediately to get up and shift for himself, for Mr Moodie, with a great number of redcoats, had landed in the island, and were hastening towards Burray to burn the house, etc. Upon which Mr Taylor made ready to get from the house, and when he had gone out of the close, saw Sir James and his brother in law, Mr Carmichael, running towards the old barnyards, but had not got a furlong from the house, when Moodie with his party surpriz'd them, and apprehended Sir James, but Mr Carmichael got off by speed of foot.

Mr Taylor and William Watt, merchant in Kirkwall, made all the haste they could towards the Little Ferry, but on their way thither they were advis'd that some of

Moodie's people, detach'd for that end, had broke the boats lying near the store house, which made them turn towards the east end of the Island, and on their way applied to one of Sir James's tenants to carry them about Burrayhead to South Ronaldsay in a boat which was lying near to the kirk, promising him a very large reward. But he stifly refused to gratify them, tho' he might have done it with all ease and safety, being a consummate coward and traitor, as the bulk of his neighbours commonly are. This necessitate them to proceed further eastward to the rocks within the East park where they might have probably lien conceal'd till the redcoats had withdrawn from the Isle. But Mr Taylor being confident of his having acted all along in so cautious and irreprehensible a manner that he could neither be apprehended nor imprison'd by any British law in being, left the rocks and walked westward, and within a few minutes Mr Watt and he were surprized by two of Mr Moodie's men arm'd with musquets, pistols and swords, who, with many others, were now traversing the whole Isle in quest of Mr Carmichael, who was lurking in a tenant's house, but basely betray'd and catch'd by the pursuers, and carried to the house of Burray, where Master Taylor and Watt were confin'd under a guard some time before.

Sir James was, immediately after being apprehended, hurried away under a guard of soldiers to a boat, and carried to a tender anchor'd in Holm Sound, to which Messieurs Carmichael, Taylor and Watt were caried some few hours thereafter . . .

Sir James and his three fellow captives continu'd on the cutter till 'twas determin'd by Messieurs Moodie and Ross to have them carried to the Tolbooth of Kirkwall, in pursuance of which resolve they were landed after seven at night, and oblig'd to travel to the burgh aforesaid, guarded by all Moodie's command, who, with Mr Ross, strutted before them all the way like two bashaws after some remarkable victory. When they enter'd the town they were met by the train'd bands of Kirkwall, who made no small and martial an appearance, and were kept for some time in the streets to display the glories of the young hero's triumph and to gratify the malice of the Mortonian faction, who, like heedless asses, implicitly followed the subverter of their interest and liberties, and, indeed, mortally hated Sir James, yea, and all that oppos'd their follies or tender'd the good of their country without a cause. After this parade they were carried into the town house and guards plac'd within, and around it without, where they were lodg'd till about four of the clock the next afternoon, when they were taken out and carried in triumph through the streets and led on their way for Stromness, which lies about twelve miles from the burgh.

Some of the poor redcoats who had slept very little for two days before, and had drunk somewhat too much, which had render'd them incapable to march on foot, were soundly drub'd by Moodie with his feet and pike till he broke the last over one of their heads. Fine discipline this for brave military men! And he forgot not to add weight to the correction by loud magnanimous curses and horrid imprecations.

The prisoners came to Alexander Graham's house in Stromness about ten at night, and were allow'd to take a small refreshment. During which time a poor man, of the name of Johnstone, had come in to see Sir James Steuart, and was mournfully condoling his present confinement, which, Mr Moodie hearing, enter'd the room in a hideous fury, curs'd and unmercifully beat him with his feet, till the poor old man fell to the floor. And immediately the four captives were hurried to a boat and carried to the *Shark* sloop of war commanded by Mr Middleton, then lying off Stromness. This gentleman is famous for his faithful services done to some English

73

merchants by whom he had been employed some years before to find out the north-west passage. And here they were confin'd under many hardships and indignities till the 11th or 12th of June, when they were turn'd over to the *Old Loo* man of war, commanded by an English gentleman, Captain Noreberry, who us'd them with the greatest humanity and kindness.

On the first day of July Sir James Steuart and his three fellow-prisoners were turn'd over from the *Old Loo* to the *Terror* sloop, commanded by Mr Duff, son to Patrick Duff, sometime Laird of Craigstown in Buchan. Good Captain Noreberry sent his first lieutenant, Mr Manwaring, along with them, desiring him to inform Mr Duff how they had been treat by him while on board the *Loo*, and to tell him that whatever civilities he should show to them he would resent as done to himself. To which the haughty Duff paid very small regard.

Within some hours after they came to this sloop, they were, by the great indulgence of their new captain, coop'd up in an ugly hole of about six foot long and somewhat less in breadth, where they suffer'd extremely for many weeks; nor could a Turkish bashaw have born himself higher towards these prisoners than the young officer did towards them while under his command.

This sloop loos'd from the Island of Barra on the third day of July, where the crew had done all the mischief they could, and within three days was on the coast of Buchan opposite to Rosantie, and the next day was opposite to Banff, where the brave captain went ashore to visit some of his near relations. That afternoon she made for Cromarty Road where she anchor'd and continu'd for some days, whence she was order'd to the road of Inverness, and there lay at anchor till the first of August, when she sail'd as a convoy to the *Pamela* of Barrowstownness, then a transport in the Government's service, on board of which were several scores of prisoners who (poor men!) had each of them the allowance of half a pound oat meal, such as it was, a day, and a chopin [*about a quart*] of water. On the seventh they anchor'd on the Thames opposite to Woolwich, and the ninth, Sir James was carried by a messenger to New-prison, where he was clapt in irons, soon after fever'd, and died within a week or two. . . .

After Sir James was carried from the *Terror*, the three remaining prisoners were more harshly us'd than ever before. For tho' the hold to which they were confin'd had neither air nor light but from the door, and very little of either that way, their humane countryman, the tender hearted Captain, commanded the door to be shut and padlock'd upon them about eighth at night, and not to be opened till after eighth in the morning. And besides, two centinels were plac'd at the door with swords and pistols for the more security. In this situation Master Taylor was often necessitate to suck in air through the chinks of the door to prevent being stifled. Some days being spent under these new hardships, they were turn'd over to the formention'd *Pamela*, where many of the poor prisoners had died, and their bodies were thrown into the river. But the dead after this were interr'd at the charge of the inhabitants of Woolwich. Many were still heavily sick, and it was dangerous to be shut up in the hold with them. Here the three foresaid captives met with MacNeil of Barra and Young Glenbucket, who had been brought prisoners on the *Pamela* from Inverness.

Conditions aboard the Pamela *may be judged from the report of a medical officer, Mr Minshaw, instructed to inspect her by the Commissioners for Wounded:*

'*Report of Mr Minshaw as to state of Rebel Prisoners on Board* Pamela *at Woolwich*
'On Thursday night the 20th August 1746 between 8 and

9 o'clock I went on board the vessel called the *Pamela*, saw the commanding officer of the Guard over the prisoners, who appointed next morning at 6 to inspect the prisoners to take account of their names, etc. At which time I attended, and, on my looking down into the hold where the prisoners then were, was saluted with such an intolerable smell that it was like to overcome me, tho' I was provided with proper herbs and my nostrils stuffed therewith. After seating ourselves on the quarter deck the prisoners were called up one by one, such as were able to come, and on being asked told their names, in what regiment or corps they served, of what age they were and where born. The number of those who came on deck were 54, many of whom were very ill as appeared by their countenance and their snail creep pace in ascending the ladder, being only just able to crawl up.

'18 who were left below were said to be utterly incapable of coming up on deck unless by the help of a string [*sling?*] which was not thought necessary as two of the most hardy of the Guard went down into the Hold, and took an account of their names etc., a fair copy of which, as well as the list taken above deck, I would have transcribed, but the commanding officer who wrote the List taken above chose to do it himself and send it as mentioned in his letter.

'To hear the description given by the Guard who went into the Hold of the uncleanliness of that place is surpassing imagination, and too nautious to describe, so that that, together with the malignant fever raging amonst them, and another odious distemper peculiar to Scotchmen, may terminate in a more dreadful disease.'

On the 24th, the *Pamela* was order'd down the river to anchor between Gravesend and Tilburry Fort, where some other transports were lying with prisoners, which was no convenient station for people so confin'd, for the country on each side the river is very wet and marshy, which occasions frequent unwholesome fogs, and all the grand necessaries of life sell there at a much higher rate than in many places in England.

At length by the indulgence of the Court every prisoner was allow'd half a pound weight of bread a day, and an quarter of an pound weight of cheese or butter for breakfast, and on the flesh days half an pound boil'd beef for dinner, but no ale or beer. But by the avarice and villainy of the victualler, one Bonny, a broken taylor, they seldom or never receiv'd above three-fourths of the said weights, and sometimes not so much. Besides, it was the opinion of many that the fleshes were none of the wholesomest kind, as being purchased from butchers who were suspected to deal in diseased cattle. But they were oblig'd to use such victuals or starve. And even such of the prisoners as had money were greatly straitned to obtain healthy provisions by the boundless avarice of the soldiers and backwardness of the sailors to bring them honestly from Gravesend.

Upon the night of [?] of September, Master Carmichael made his escape by getting out at the cabbin window, falling into the river, by which he was born up by four bladders which, it seems, he prepared for that end, and was carried to the Southwark side whence he got safe to London, and there remain'd in the safest way he could till after the Act of Indemnity was publish'd in Summer 1747.

Mr Taylor survived to write, in 1750, the third-person account from which this description is taken. Only fifty-eight prisoners escaped from captivity in the wholesale programme of arrest and imprisonment and transportation which followed the defeat at Culloden – forty-five from Scotland, thirteen from England. Carmichael's is the only recorded escape from the transports.

6

The Escape of Midshipman
Donat Henchy O'Brien, R.N.
from the fortress of Bitche in France
during the Napoleonic Wars,
14th September, 1807

Donat Henchy O'Brien entered the Royal Navy on 16th December, 1796, as a midshipman. He was then eleven years old. On 10th February, 1804, he was taken prisoner by the French when HMS Hussar, aboard which he was serving, was wrecked off the Saintes. He was imprisoned at Givet from 28th March until 16th July, 1804; then transferred to Verdun, whence he escaped on 28th August, 1807. Recaptured on 18th September, 1807, he was dispatched to the 'Colditz' of these wars, the massive fortress of Bitche in north-east France. He escaped en route, but was recaptured and arrived at Bitche, in chains, in the winter of 1807. His reputation had preceded him. 'You deserve the severest punishment,' the commandant told him, 'for not resting quietly with your guards, and for being accessory to the punishment of them.' O'Brien replied that he 'was conscious that I had only done my duty in endeavouring to escape.'

I shall not attempt to describe the fortress of Bitche. To give a minute detail of its strength, *souterrains*, etc., would fill a volume. At this moment it is sufficient for me to say that it is reckoned one of the strongest fortifications of

France, and is built on the summit of an immensely high rock, out of which all its subterranean caves are hollowed. It has, on one side, three ramparts. The first is from ninety to one hundred feet high; the second, from forty to fifty; and the third, from twenty-five to thirty, with redoubts, entrenchments, and all contrivances of military engineering, almost innumerable. As I surveyed these stupendous heights and depths, it appeared to me a physical impossibility to escape from it, and I was filled with despair. Nothing but madness could entertain a thought of attempting to escape. Being now arrived at the wretched dungeon I was to inhabit, my handcuffs and chains were taken off, and the Corsican deserters were conducted to the condemned cells. They were, I believe, soon afterwards shot. A dismal dungeon was unlocked, in which it seemed that I was doomed to be entombed alive. Solitude appeared to me dreadful, and I looked upon a 'living death' as my final lot; but I found in the dungeon Mr Worth, midshipman, and a Captain Brine of the merchant service. The latter was one of those who came from Verdun with me. They were on a door, which they had managed to unhinge, and which lay as a platform to keep them out of the excrement and wet, that were more than ankle deep: they had a little straw and a blanket. They informed me, they had been companions of the unfortunate Essel in the late attempt to get over the ramparts. Six of them had broken out of their cave, had got a rope made of sheets, and were on the point of lowering themselves down, when they were discovered and the alarm given, which made four of them clap on the rope together, though only strong enough to lower one at a time, or two at most; the rope, in consequence, broke. One [*Lt Essel*] was dashed to pieces, and the three others – I think their names were Nason, Potts, and Adams – so severely mangled and bruised that little hopes were at first entertained of their recovery; Worth and Brine were soon seized by the guards on the embrasure. The others were then improving fast, and they expected them in the dungeon in a few days, as soon as the surgeon had reported them well enough; after which they would have to remain in this receptacle of filth for thirty-one days, which was the usual time of being buried alive in the first and most horrible gradation of our captivity. It was fifty deep stone steps under ground, for I have often counted them, and the most dark and intricate passages led from it to the gaoler's house, who had the watching and superintending of the prisoners, in conjunction with a guard.

We now again began to devise and meditate upon plans for escaping. One proposed undermining the dungeon. I saw no prospect whatever of succeeding in this point. I, however, was willing to try every means to regain my liberty. Hammers and chisels with great difficulty were procured, and we carried them always about us, as the dungeon was ransacked every day in our absence. We hung an old coat up against that part of the rock which we intended to begin upon. Rope was necessary to descend the ramparts after we had got out of the dungeon; we accordingly, through some friends, who had obtained permission to come and see us, contrived to purchase some stout linen for shirts (which we really much wanted), and from the shoemakers amongst the prisoners we got, now and then, a ball of twine. We procured needles, bees'-wax, etc., by degrees, and made a rope of four or five fathoms for each, which we *marled* with the remainder of the twine, and passed tight round our bodies underneath the shirt. Our working time commenced immediately on being locked up after breathing the fresh air. Night would not do, as it would be necessary to have candle-light, and we might have been seen through the bars by our sentinels.

The undermining business was found impracticable, and was consequently dropped. Having a rope, we flattered ourselves we might, some day whilst allowed to breathe the fresh air, be able to elude the vigilance of the sentinels and scale the walls. However, this proved to be a plan so difficult to accomplish that it was abandoned, and our only hope was that we might have an opportunity of using the rope when we should be liberated from our present dungeon and placed in another *souterrain* or apartment of the fortress.

An attempt to break out on 17th July, 1808, was foiled and those captured were taken off to court martial. O'Brien was implicated in this attempt but was not caught in the act; and two months later, with three companions – Hewson, Barklimore and Batley – tried a new plan.

It was now the 13th of September, and the third day since my friend Hewson had joined us. The night was very boisterous and inclement, and this we thought proved much in our favour. Everything was got ready. Our rope was tightly wound into a ball and concealed in a pocket handkerchief. Every moment was anxiously watched and counted. At length darkness set in. It rained in torrents, blew almost a hurricane, the thunder rolled with a tremendous sound, and I scarcely ever witnessed in any part of the globe a more desperate night. All this was so far, we considered, propitious; but, unfortunately, the flashes of lightning were vivid and incessant, and this was a serious source of danger.

We now unlocked our door, and remained at the bottom of the flight of stairs, waiting to see the sentinels go into their boxes. This was about eight o'clock, and four hours did we watch, until midnight, and not a single soul of them left his post. This was the more provoking, for as it poured a deluge of rain, and they were without their greatcoats, we had calculated with certainty upon their requiring and seeking shelter. The reverse was the case, and during the whole time they were as vigilant as if they had suspected our designs.

We at last agreed to return to our apartments until the ensuing night, and to deposit all our apparatus in places we had previously fixed upon for concealment; but, upon second thoughts, we considered that, in all probability, the sentinels that came to relieve the watch at midnight would not be so very hardy or watchful as their predecessors, and that we might yet have an opportunity of putting our scheme into execution. In this expectation or hope we waited, in a state of intense anxiety, until two in the morning; but, to our discomfiture, we found that the sentinels defied the elements, and kept their posts in the strictest sense of duty. Chagrined and vexed, we returned to our apartments, locked the door and went to bed.

The *souterrain* was opened at the usual hour, and our friends came running up, imagining, from the inclemency of the night, that we must have succeeded in effecting our escape; and greatly were they disappointed at finding us all snug in our beds. I related all the circumstances to them: they shrugged up their shoulders, and expressed their fears that, if we could not get off in such a night as the last, there was little hope of our escaping in fair weather.

On the 14th September we dined early, that we might have the pleasure of our friends' company to a farewell dinner during the time allowed them for breathing the fresh air. We were determined to lay in a good foundation for our journey, and got a very large piece of beef, had it roasted, and procured plenty of bread, beer, and vegetables. This, for our circumstances, was more than an alderman's feast: we all enjoyed it, earnestly hoping that it might be the last that we should ever eat within the walls of a French prison. Our friends pointed out to us the number of difficulties we should have to surmount in passing the guards – the danger that would attend it – and expressed the anxiety they were under for us. We, however, were determined not to relinquish our undertaking, and to be ready every night until an opportunity offered. We parted as we had done the night before. They did not suppose we should have any chance that night, as the weather was moderate and fair. At our usual hour of six (the winter regulations having commenced) we were locked up, and immediately recommenced our preparations. We thought, perhaps, the sentinels might be more careless early in the evening; that is to say, before eight, which was the usual time to set the night-watch and give the necessary orders.

We were now again all ready. Our door was opened; and we could see the sentinel, whom we had most to fear, walk up and down before our windows. His box was in front of the door, in the yard through which we had to go; but, as our guards lived underneath our apartments, we thought he would take anybody moving about so early for one of them: and it was unusual to challenge anyone before eight o'clock.

At about seven, the soldier, to our infinite joy, entered his box. I instantly descended the stairs that led into the yard. It was just dusk; and I was to take six minutes on the forlorn hope, as it might justly be termed, to fix our rope to a palisade, and to descend the first rampart, before Mr Hewson followed, who was next on the list. I passed the sentinel quite close, and could see him leaning over his musket. He never moved, though I met his eye, probably taking me for one of the guards; and I arrived, providentially, at the spot fixed upon to make fast the rope, which I very soon accomplished, and was just in the act of descending when my friend Hewson arrived. In a few minutes, to my inexpressible satisfaction, we were all four at the bottom of the first wall. Our principal object being now accomplished, we congratulated each other. We had two walls yet to descend; the heights, as I have already mentioned, being respectively from ninety to one hundred, from forty to fifty, and the third from twenty-five to thirty feet. We all clapped on to the rope, and crawled up with our feet against the wall, until we got a good height. We then swung off together, when the rope broke, and we fell upon one another, leaving in our hands enough to enable us to descend the next rampart. We made this piece fast to one of the upper stones of the embrasure, and again descended. We had now to repeat our haul upon the rope, and it again broke, leaving a piece of sufficient length for our future purpose, the descent of the third and last rampart.

We had taken the precaution of providing two long boot-hooks to stick in the wall, to make our rope fast to, in case we should find no other means of securing it. These proved of the greatest use in getting down the third rampart. In fact, had we not had them with us, we must have surrendered ourselves, for not one single means could we find of fastening the rope to anything, and to drop from a height of thirty feet might have been destruction. The boot-hooks served our purpose: we were at the bottom of the third wall; and all that we had now to do was to pass the outer sentinels, who were few in number, and rather slack in vigilance, perhaps from the supposed impossibility of any prisoner effecting an escape in this direction. We had, in fact, let ourselves down by this frail rope a total height of from about 180 to 200 feet.

At the bottom of the third rampart we remained in the *fosse* or ditch; and we had to watch the turn of the sentinel that was pacing immediately before us. As soon as his back was fairly turned, we ascended the scarp of the ditch, and gently rolled ourselves down the slope or glacis. In a few minutes, with our hearts rebounding

with joyous emotions, we were on the road to Stras-
bourg, on which we continued running as fast as we
possibly could for nearly an hour. We then halted to put
on our shoes, which we had hung round our necks as we
rolled down the glacis, as we had found it more secure
to descend the walls without shoes than with them, the
feet being much more pliable.

We now turned round to take, as we hoped, a final
view of the Mansion of Tears, the name that had been so
long given to this detestable fortress by the unfortunate
prisoners, many of whom had shed an abundance, or
showers of them, within its horrid cells and dungeons.
We spontaneously returned our thanks to Almighty God
for our deliverance, and shook each other cordially by
the hand, overwhelmed with exultation at our almost
miraculous success. When we looked at the stupendous
heights of the rock and fortress, it seemed as if a miracle
alone could have enabled us to descend them, suspended
by so slight and ill-made a cord as that which we had
been able to construct out of our shirt-linen and a little
cobbler's twine.

*From Bitche, O'Brien and his companions headed east, stole a
boat, and crossed the Rhine. Batley was ill and growing worse,
so they had eventually to leave him in an inn near Rastadt,
where he was later recaptured. Led by O'Brien, the other three
turned south through Baden, Offenburg and Hornberg, and then
east through Bavaria into Austria; the frontier officials politely
accepted the fiction that these three travellers were 'American
citizens'. Safe from recapture they travelled south to Trieste and
arrived on 4th November, 1808, to see the Royal Navy frigate
HMS Unité blockading the port. 'Our concealment in woods
and terrors at towns, our swampy beds, drenched backs, and
starved stomachs, were most pleasurable reminiscences, when we
felt that they had led us to the 'high top gallant of our joy' and
that we now saw our glorious element, with a little frigate under*

old England's flag blockading the port and keeping the whole line of coast in awe.' On the morning of 8th November, 1808, they boarded HMS Amphion, which had arrived to take over from Unité, and 'had the happiness of being once more under our proper colours and on our own element'. Sent to Malta, O'Brien had the further joy of meeting Mr Batley, who had escaped again following his recapture at Rastadt and had made his own way to Trieste. After him, in their turn, came five old friends from Bitche, to whom O'Brien had written in German, setting out the escape route; the letter, being in German, had been handed over unread by the guards. 'The French considered Bitche their stronghold for English prisoners,' he wrote proudly, 'and greatly must they have been annoyed and mortified by so many having triumphed over their force, ingenuity and vigilance.'

O'Brien achieved his lieutenancy that spring and was appointed commander in 1813. For him, however, the ending of the Napoleonic wars meant the close of all adventures; he lived out most of the rest of his life in enforced retirement from the sea, dying as a rear-admiral in 1857.

7

The Escape of Lieutenant James Wells, from the Confederate Prison in Richmond, Virginia, during the American Civil War, 9th February, 1864

James Wells, a second-lieutenant in the 8th Michigan Cavalry, was captured by the Confederate forces and sent to Libby Prison, which at that time held 1200 officers. When first he saw the prison, he wrote, a quotation came into his mind: 'All hope abandon, ye who enter here.'

Libby Prison, at the time of which I write, was situated between Cary and Canal Streets, in the city of Richmond, Virginia, the width of the building extending one hundred and ten feet from one street to the other, its sides running along either street one hundred and forty feet east and west. It was three stories high on Cary Street, with a basement cellar under the centre of the building, making it four stories high on Canal Street.

Across the width of the building, extending from the basement to the roof, were two partition walls, dividing each floor into three rooms, or apartments, of equal size. Our prisoners at this time occupied the two upper floors, or the six upper rooms. The rooms were designated as the upper and lower east rooms, the upper and lower middle rooms, and the upper and lower west rooms. The middle room on the first [*ground*] floor below was used for cooking purposes and was known as the 'kitchen'. It had three fireplaces in its east partition wall. This kitchen was the only place in the building the prisoners had free access to, save the six rooms spoken of above. The fireplaces were not utilised, but in front of each one of them were three stoves, the pipes of which went into the chimney flues running upward above the fireplaces. The flues did not extend below this floor, so the partition wall from here down was solid. The east room on the first floor was used for hospital purposes; the west room was the office where the prison officials were quartered, and the basement beneath was divided up into dungeons for the confinement and punishment of unruly prisoners. The doors and windows of the prison were barred like those of a jail.

Aside from the effects of hunger, there was a feeling of unrest among many of the prisoners which, if yielded to, often led to serious despondency and even insanity. Plan after plan was devised for escape, only to be proved impracticable. In the dead hours of the night men could be seen prowling around the prison, in the hope that some means of escape might offer.

By their continued movements at night the prisoners most desirous of escape gradually came to know each other and to take counsel together, and in this way a compact association consisting of only fifteen men was formed in Libby, and tunnelling was decided upon. An effort to go out through a large sewer was abandoned as impracticable after considerable time and labour had been lost.

It was finally determined to begin in the basement under the east end of the building, a place familiarly known among the prisoners as 'rat hell', and tunnel eastward, coming out under a carriage-shed attached to a large building on the opposite side of the street, where the escaping prisoners could lie screened from the observation of the guards around the prison behind a high board fence, extending from the ground to the roof of the shed, until they found it safe to emerge. The tunnel was to run under a short cross street reaching from Canal to Cary Street, at the east end of the prison.

But how was this cellar, which was to form the base of all operations, to be reached? The prisoners could not go into the hospital room and thence through the floor into the cellar, for in this room were nurses and guards who would at once discover the plan. They could not go into the basement, under the cook-room, and then through the partition wall into the east basement for there were guards on duty there all the time. Every step taken had to be kept a profound secret, not only from the Confederate authorities but from the majority of the prisoners also; and until secure access to the cellar could be obtained nothing could be done.

It was finally determined to go behind the stoves in one of the fireplaces just described and, taking out the bricks in the centre, follow the partition wall down below the floor on which the cook and hospital rooms were located, a distance of three or four feet, and then go through the wall into the cellar, thus escaping observation from every quarter. This was successfully accomplished. Major A. J. Hamilton, of the Eleventh Kentucky Cavalry, was the author of this plan, while Thomas E. Rose, later of the Sixteenth U.S. Infantry, then colonel of the Seventy-seventh Pennsylvania Volunteers, was the chief engineer of all tunnelling operations and the leading spirit of the entire enterprise.

Beginning in the fireplace, then, the bricks were removed from the centre of the wall, so as to make an opening wide enough to admit a man's body. From fifty to seventy-five bricks were taken out. The work was all accomplished secretly and at night. After 'lights out' or nine o'clock, at which time everybody in the prison was supposed to be lying down, two men, having first quietly removed the bricks, would go down and take turns with each other in digging throughout the night. In the meantime two or three others, detailed for that purpose, would remain on watch in different parts of the prison and be ready to give the signal and help the two workmen up on the first approach of day. The night's work done, the bricks were carefully replaced, covered over with soot and dirt which was always plentiful behind the stoves, and in this condition the place was left secure from observation until night came on again. This operation was repeated nearly every night for about seven weeks.

The authorities made regular tours of inspection through the prison every day, while hundreds of prisoners were in this room and about these stoves, engaged in cooking from early morning till nine o'clock at night, and yet not more than twenty or twenty-five men ever knew of the work until it was nearly all accomplished. From the bottom of the cellar an opening was first made through the stone wall, some four or five feet thick, and then the work of excavating began. Clam shells and case-knives were the principal tools used, and with these simple instruments a tunnel sixteen inches in diameter, eight or nine feet below the surface of the ground and about sixty feet long, was dug.

As the work progressed, difficulty in removing the dirt from the tunnel was experienced. To overcome this, a spittoon from one of the rooms above – a box about eight inches square and five inches deep – was taken down into the cellar; and the man digging inside would pull the box in by means of a cord attached to one side and, after filling it with dirt, give a signal, when the man in the cellar, by another string, would pull it out and empty it. By this slow and wearisome process the whole mass of dirt was removed.

The back end of the cellar or basement was not used by the authorities and was seldom invaded by any person or thing except rats; but it was filled several feet deep with straw which had been placed there for hospital purposes, though not in use at that time. As the dirt from the tunnel came out it was spread evenly over the bottom of the cellar and covered with this straw, thus concealing it from observation through the day. The front part of the cellar was used as a store-room, and attachés of the prison were in and out by day, but seldom if ever at night.

When the tunnel had reached a distance of twenty feet the air became so foul that one man had to fan at the open mouth while the other man dug. So foul was it at times that a candle would not burn; yet to dig successfully light was found to be a necessity as well as air. Lights were obtained by stealthily taking a portion of the candles furnished to the various rooms each night.

Those who had been let into the secret of the tunnel now began to put themselves in readiness for the exodus, which they f saw would mark the beginning of their greatest trials. To harden our limbs and muscles persistent and continued walking and other physical exercises were resorted to. My comrade and myself once walked a distance of twenty-two miles around the room in a single day. I was nearly barefooted and for a long time had my eye on a pair of boots belonging to one Lieutenant Mead of a Union Kentucky Regiment. I had received a box from home and had offered Mead many of my choicest things for his boots, for boots I must have before making the escape. But Mead, who knew nothing of the tunnel or the special purpose for which the boots were wanted, was inexorable. I had often tried them on to show how well they fitted me – even better, I thought, than they fitted Mead – but to no effect; it was no go. When the night came for the escape I lay down by Mead's side according to my custom and as if for the usual night's rest. An hour had not passed before Mead was wrapped in profound slumber, when I pulled on his boots and, like the Arab, folded my tent and silently stole away. I still lacked a hat; but in passing out among my sleeping comrades I stumbled upon one belonging to Lieutenant Thomas McKee of the First West Virginia Regiment, who nightly shared the luxuries of the floor with me in that immediate neighbourhood, and, without compunction or further ceremony, I hurriedly placed it where, in my own judgement at least, it would do the most good.

There was no way of judging the distance across the street under which the tunnel ran, save as it was measured by the eye from the windows above. So, when the tunnel had been carried far enough, as was believed, to reach the carriage-shed, it was thought best by those in charge of the digging to prospect by means of a small hole dug upward for the purpose. The men engaged below that night commenced running up at an angle of forty-five degrees. A short time before this some workmen had been employed in the prison, making repairs and strengthening the doors and windows. It was their custom to leave their tools in the prison overnight and these, used by them for fastening our chains, were now made use of by the tunnelling party in cutting them loose; for, one night, from the carpenter's outfit, our fellows stole an augur and chisel and carried them down into the cellar for use in that quarter, and they were for ever lost to the Confederacy though they did good service in forwarding our escape. I believe the chisel was the principal tool in use that night the prospecting hole was made. The man engaged in digging was reaching ahead into the small opening, letting the dirt rattle back down the inclined plane, when suddenly the chisel went through the surface at a point full in the glare of a street lamp, and not more than ten or twelve paces from where a sentinel walked. The noise made by the chisel as it went through was heard by a guard who asked another nearby if he had heard the noise. He replied, 'Yes,' but that it was 'nothing but rats', and both walked on. Their conversation was plainly overheard by the real 'rat' under the ground. The hole was at once stopped up with little stones and whatever material could be utilised for the purpose, and the main tunnel went on some ten or fifteen feet further.

The plan was, when the tunnel should be completed, to let as many prisoners into the secret as could well get out in a single night, and then, leaving it to someone behind to cover up the excavations in the wall and so preventing the discovery of the tunnel by the Confederates, let as many more escape at another time.

On the night of the 9th of February 1864, everything being in readiness, about two hundred men who at this time had been let into the secret were assembled in the cook-room after nine o'clock, ready to take the desperate chances of escape. It was a trying moment. The digging of the tunnel had been a gigantic undertaking, accompanied with the greatest anxiety, hardship and privation; and now, completed at last, it only opened the way to dangers no man of us could forecast.

About a dozen or fifteen men had gone down through the hole in the wall into the cellar and my turn had just come, when a noise at the outside door caused a report to be circulated that those who had gone out had been recaptured and that the guards were coming in to take us all under arrest. This was made the signal for a general stampede across the room, a distance of one hundred and ten feet, to the stairway in the corner leading up to the rooms where the prisoners belonged. My partner, who was equipped with a haversack containing a scant supply of rations saved for the occasion and a map of the country which we had drawn up with a pencil, ran back with the crowd. I remained behind the stoves and reflected a minute. Listening at the door, I could hear no one coming in. 'And if they do,' said I to myself, 'they know nothing of this hole and nothing of the tunnel, and anyhow I may just as well go down and out; it can be no worse for me.' Accordingly down through the hole in the wall I went.

On reaching the tunnel I found a young man by the name of White, a lieutenant from Erie, Pennsylvania, just going in. He said, 'Wells, I will wait for you at the shed'. I waited until he had made his way through, for, on account of the foul air, it was dangerous for more than one to enter the tunnel at once. I was soon through, dragging my overcoat on my legs behind me. I found on emerging that White had gone and that I was alone. I stretched myself up at full length and breathed the fresh air for the first time in six long months. I felt the soft ground under my feet, and looked over and about me as if to assure myself that it was not all a dream. I never felt a greater determination to accomplish a purpose in my life, and resolved to push on and by continued efforts realise the benefits of the labours already performed, or perish in the attempt. My nerves were strung to the highest tension. All fear had vanished, and my senses were as alert and quick as those of a wild animal.

From the shed we had to pass through a gate which opened on Canal Street. Along this street, to within twenty steps of the gate, a sentinel walked, who on reaching a certain point would face about and go a distance of forty or sixty paces the other way. Taking advantage of the time when his back was turned, the prisoners opened the gate and, stepping out on Canal Street, passed out of sight. In this manner all emerged from the gate, one by one, or sometimes in parties of two or three. The alarm causing the prisoners to stampede from the cook-room proved to be a false one, and that night one hundred and nine men got out. Among the number was my partner, but after five days he was recaptured. Of the whole number who went through the tunnel only forty-eight got entirely away.

Watching my opportunity, I slipped out in the manner just described and walked two squares down Canal Street. I had no fixed plan for getting out of the city but was guided wholly by impulse and by circumstances as they were presented, though my general purpose was, by some means, if possible, to place the Chickahominy River, which to the northward was not more than six miles distant, between myself and Richmond that night. My especial object in this was to baffle any pursuit that might be made with dogs.

The Federal uniform which I wore was rather an advantage to me than otherwise, for the Confederate soldiers had appropriated clothing sent by our Government, and were then commonly wearing our uniforms on the streets. After reaching the borders of the city, out of reach of the street lamps, I took the centre of the road and made my way as quietly and rapidly as possible.

Presently I came into a dense thicket on low bottom-land, covered here and there with water. I believed myself near the Chickahominy. Coming to some flood wood on the edge of a considerable body of water as black as midnight, I broke off a large piece of the light-coloured bark and threw it into the water, deeming that if it floated off the water was that of the river. It did float off, and immediately I proceeded to place the stream between myself and Richmond. In doing this, however, I had to wade in water and mud waist deep.

I had barely reached the uplands on the north side when daylight came on, and I at once sought a hiding-place for the day. This I found a little further on, by crawling inside an old inclosure which had grown up to a dense thicket of laurel and other brush. As the day approached, I could hear the voices of the Confederate soldiers encamped near the river a half-mile away. About nine or ten o'clock I heard a body of cavalry coming up the road from the direction of Richmond and, standing up, could just see their heads as they passed on the gallop, not more than two hundred yards distant.

These men, as I readily divined, were in pursuit of escaped prisoners, for that morning at the accustomed roll-call one hundred and nine men had failed to put in their appearance, and dogs were at once brought into requisition to hunt down the fugitives. A rigorous search was also instituted to discover, if possible, the means of our escape; but some of our men, by previous arrangement, took the precaution to stop up the places of egress, at the same time prying off a bar from the window and hanging out a rope made by tying together strips of blankets. This ruse led the authorities to suppose we had escaped through the window, having first bribed the guards. This deceived them for a while, and the guards and officers on duty were arrested and sent to the guard-house, all the while protesting their innocence. Search was then made throughout the day, and it was not until nearly nightfall that a coloured boy, chancing to go into the shed, discovered the hole where we had emerged; but for many days thereafter they did not learn how we went into the cellar from the cook-room.

Wells lay hidden all day and walked on through the night, surviving an encounter with a late-night walker.

Towards morning I came to a crossroads where there was a mile-post and finger-board. I climbed the post and, holding on by one hand, with the other struck a match which I had carried in my pocket for a long time. On the board was an index finger pointing nearly in the direction I had been travelling for the past two hours, and beneath it the words 'Twelve miles to Richmond'. I had then travelled the greater part of two nights and made but twelve miles. By this time hunger and fatigue and loss of sleep were closing in upon me with a deathlike grip. I pushed on however, though from sheer exhaustion often stumbling and falling to the ground. In going through an open woodland I suddenly came upon an encampment of Confederate teamsters, doubtless a quartermaster's train carrying provisions to the army about Richmond. Some of the men were up knocking about among the mules and wagons. It very dark. Assuming the rôle of a driver and bursting out in the vernacular common to the class, I walked up to a mule and gave him a kick in the ribs, and in a gruff voice commanded him to 'Stand around'. Repeating this and similar operations two or three times, I soon, without interruption, made my way through the encampment.

When morning came I again sought a hiding-place. Shivering and hungry throughout that day, and unable to move for fear of detection, I had a good opportunity to reflect upon the mutability of human affairs and the vicissitudes of a soldier's life. Night coming on, I again took my bearings and was about to start out when I overheard footsteps in the brush not far distant and, crouching down like a frightened rabbit, awaited developments. Nearer and nearer the steps came. I thought I had been discovered and that my time had come, for now I could distinguish the steps of two persons. Soon into plain sight, almost on tiptoe, walked two escaped prisoners, McCain, of the Twenty-first Illinois, and Randall, of the Second Ohio Regiment. I recognised them at once and I hailed them in a whisper. They shared with me from their scant rations of corn bread, and then, for the first time in thirty-six hours, I tasted

97

food. We here travelled on together; and once or twice during the remainder of the week we obtained provisions of coloured men, who were true to the escaped prisoners in every instance.

We had been travelling four nights, all the time in the woods, and Sunday morning found us well-nigh exhausted. We came to the conclusion that it would be impossible to travel in that way any longer and so, after lying down for an hour or more for a little rest, we started out for the first time by daylight. Following up a ravine, we soon came out into an open field inside of which was a schoolhouse or church, and people, evidently attending service, had already begun to assemble. Beyond ran a road which forked near the schoolhouse, and not more than one hundred and fifty yards from our hiding-place in the brush. Two or three little dogs came uncomfortably near and, while we were debating what course to pursue, about seventy-five cavalrymen rode by and halted at the fork of the Road. Randall volunteered to crawl around to the road below the school, to see if it were possible for us to cross in that direction unobserved. He disappeared in the brush and we never saw him again, but the report of three or four guns fired down the road in the direction he had taken led us to suppose he had been shot and killed. One of the dogs now discovered McCain and myself, and commenced barking furiously. We started back down the ravine, keeping as far as possible under cover of the brush. The firing below and the barking of the dog had set the soldiers and everybody else on the *qui vive*. We were discovered in our flight and pursued by cavalrymen, but finally eluded them. Through the rest of the day we remained in the swamp, closely secreted, being fully satisfied with our experience in trying to travel by daylight. When night came on the weary march was resumed.

Coming to an opening, we discovered, some distance off, a man standing in the doorway of a cabin. Believing him to be coloured we had little hesitancy in approaching him; but on coming to within a few paces, we found him to be a white man. It was then too late to back out, and putting on a bold front we walked up and asked him for something to eat, telling him at the same time that we were Yankee prisoners recently escaped from Libby Prison, and that we were likely to perish for want of food. He told us that he had already heard of the escape, that he had been a Confederate soldier, and that he knew something of the life of a soldier. 'But,' said he, 'I never turned a hungry man away from my door yet, and do not propose to do so now.' Whereupon, by his invitation, we followed him into the house. He gave us three or four dry biscuits, stating that they constituted his whole store of provisions. He appeared friendly and kind from the start, but we followed him into the house, fearing he might possibly bring out a musket instead of meat. He even directed us which way to go to avoid detection and capture, and told us that we were only a short distance from the York River, where a gunboat flying the American flag had passed down not more than an hour before.

Our objective point now was Yorktown, or Williamsburg, the nearest point where our troops were stationed. We had gone a long distance out of the way and must now travel south. I had lost my hat, our clothing hung about us in rags, and all the time we were getting weaker. On the night of the seventh day out, there came a terrible storm of sleet and rain and, raking up a quantity of dry leaves by the side of a large log and covering them with boughs, we crawled under, lying closely together for shelter and warmth and rest. How long we had lain there I do not know, but presently I was awakened by McCain who said we must get up and go on or we would surely perish. I agreed with him but neither of us made an effort to rise. While lying in this state of half-stupor, I found my memory was failing me and that I could not recall my only brother's name. Suddenly, as by a concert of thought as well as action, we sprang to our feet, and soon found ourselves in an open field near a road which proved to be the Williamsburg Pike, though at the time we were in doubt as to the fact. We concluded to follow it in the direction of Williamsburg, as we believed; but, for safety, we kept back a little distance in the field. Presently we heard cavalry coming ahead of us. We had already had a little experience with Confederate cavalry and were not anxious to repeat it. But these might be our friends. We were on neutral ground, at least, and very near our own lines. It was a great risk to hail them, and a great risk to let them pass by unchallenged, for it was becoming apparent that we could not stand the pressure much longer. Approaching within a few paces of the road, we secreted ourselves in the weeds and brush. By the clatter of the iron scabbards I knew the cavalrymen were armed with sabres (it was too dark to see), and I told McCain this was to me an evidence that they belonged to our side, for the Confederate cavalry as a rule were not armed with sabres. They came up and passed on, but nothing occurred and no word was spoken to give us any clue to their identity. The situation was terrible. The cold, freezing rain was now coming down in sheets and our bones were chilled to the very marrow. The main column had got by and the rear guard, about twenty in number, were in front of us. We could endure it no longer, and resolved to hail them. Accordingly, we both stood up, and cried out, 'What regiment is that?'

As quick as thought, wheeling their horses into line along the fence, and at the same time drawing their pistols, they demanded our immediate and unconditional surrender. The click of the hammers, which we could plainly hear as they came into position, added to the horror of the moment. My hair actually stood on end. I said to McCain: 'We are gone up.' With this he seemed to agree, and replied that we had better surrender, as our lives depended upon it, and that no time was to be lost. Accordingly, we threw up our hands and together cried out, 'We will surrender.' On going to the fence we discovered that we were in the hands of a detachment of the Eleventh Pennsylvania Cavalry, which had been sent out as a rescuing party and had made every provision for our further comfort and safety.

Over fifty years later, six British officers imprisoned in Turkey were inspired by this escape to begin a tunnel of their own. Their tunnelling attempt was foiled by transfer to another camp, but they there made a second escape bid, described in Episode 11.

8

The Escape of Lieutenant J. L. Hardy, from Magdeburg P.O.W. Camp in Germany, Summer, 1916

Lieutenant Hardy, subsequently Captain Hardy, D.S.O., M.C. and bar, of the Connaught Rangers, was captured in 1914. He escaped from Augustabad in the summer of 1915, but was re-captured in Stralsund Docks and sent to Halle. He climbed out of Halle in a downpour, was again recaptured, and this time was sent to Magdeburg, where he teamed up with a Belgian officer named Baschwitz.

Hardy and Baschwitz had their eye on a small triangular courtyard in which was a roofless latrine, for orderlies only, backed against a paling. By an ingenious double-bluff they tricked the Germans into suspecting that some of the officers were planning to escape from this latrine, disguised as orderlies. The latrine was nailed up – fortunately not dismantled – and its use forbidden. Hardy and Baschwitz were delighted.

We had completed our arrangements for faking both evening and morning roll-calls for at least three days after our break-out. Baschwitz had one night placed his dummy in bed, and had then hidden himself behind a screen during roll-call. The Germans had passed it without hesitation, and this shows how perfect had been his workmanship. In my own room, on the other hand, this trick would never succeed. One solution was to make a second dummy and substitute it for another officer out of Baschwitz's room, who, in turn, would replace me in mine after I had gone. But there was no more plaster to be had, and I sadly feared that I was up against an impossibility, until one night I noticed a thing which solved the whole difficulty for me. I should have explained that these roll-calls, properly speaking, were merely a process of identification, or intended to be such, and involved no answering to one's name. The officer in charge of my room took, as I have said, the greatest care to satisfy himself that the occupant of each bed was a real live man. For three nights running I watched him, while he made his round of the room, and I came to the conclusion that neither he nor the sentries with him did more than this. *They did not count the beds*, and all I had to do was to take my bed to pieces before we left, conceal the sections and then move the others along to hide the gap.

Morning roll-call had been much more difficult to manage, but we had now arranged with two Belgian officers that they should help us. One of them lived in Baschwitz's room, the other in mine, and they both appeared to be extraordinarily decent fellows. They had nothing whatever to gain by it, and helped us out of the goodness of their hearts, and it is with the deepest regret that I have to record that both of them were eventually punished for their part in the affair. The plan was that, the morning after we had gone, they should report themselves sick and unable to attend roll-call outside. They would, however, appear on parade, but standing well back to avoid any chance of recognition. The Germans, owing to our absence, would report two officers missing, and would then be reminded that there were two sick upstairs. Roll-call being declared finished, the officer in charge would go up to the rooms to make sure that all was correct, and would find the two Belgians in bed, for they could, by entering the building through another door, just beat him by a short head. It was a very old trick to hide the absence of one prisoner by inducing the Germans unconsciously to count another man twice.

And then at last the day came, for I got up early one morning to find it raining heavily out of a grey sky. God knows if I was altogether glad. One had grown so used to looking into the future, and so accustomed to the feeling that one was *going* to escape, that one felt qualms when faced with the necessity of putting one's scheme to the test. I have known men to work for months at a time digging a tunnel under the most difficult circumstances; many became ill, but worked on; many, in spite of festering sores on knees and elbows, continued to spend five hours a day crawling about underground; all were exhausted by lack of air before the day's work was over; and yet, when the task was finished, one found a number of these men had made no preparations for their escape, and could not even nerve themselves up to take advantage of the opportunity. All this is very curious and difficult to understand, but in my opinion it does undoubtedly require a great mental effort to drive oneself on to take the plunge in these most unpleasant affairs. We had very clearly recognised, and had often discussed, the probability of one or other of us being shot while making this attempt. All sentries in this corps had instructions to fire without warning in the event of a breakout, and we expected short shrift if we were seen. I was never one of those lucky people who do not suffer from terror of sudden death or sudden mutilation, and I think that Baschwitz too knew well the meaning of fear, though a braver man I shall never meet.

We were ready before the sentry was relieved, and consequently had another ten minutes to wait. We sat there with a crowd of Baschwitz's countrymen round us, and they had a peculiarly considerate and commiserating air about them, for this is always how one feels towards a prisoner who is just about to 'go in off the deep end'. What makes *him* feel so bad is the knowledge that it is all *his* fault; that, whatever happens, he is responsible and he is to blame. This is indeed a delightful realisation should he succeed but – how often does he succeed?

'*Il est parti*,' said a friend who had been doing duty at the window.

Picking up a piece of raw bacon with which to lubricate the saw, I buttoned up my military greatcoat and followed Baschwitz and his friend downstairs. We stood waiting in the passage, well back from the door, and in this way could watch the sentry, and choose our moment without being seen by him. The sentry came out of his box and walked towards the door, and we were both trembling with excitement as we unbuttoned our greatcoats. In spite of our disguise we did not wish him to see us if it could possibly be avoided, and, as he turned to walk back, we flung our coats to the accomplice and hurried out into the yard. There were several orderlies there, and the sentry did not turn at the sound of our footsteps. We reached the latrine and I saw the men looking at us in astonishment as we scrambled over the wall and dropped inside, but they realised at once what was happening, and played up to us in fine style. My hat! what luck! if everything went as well as this first part, we should be free men within a week! And now for the job.

We knelt down and critically examined the planks through which we had to cut. They were very thick, and the little slim saw which I had procured seemed quite inadequate to the work. However, we must do our best, so I lay down on my stomach and began using one of our knives to cut a hole through which the saw could be inserted. We worked in turns for about twenty minutes before this was finished, but found to our consternation that we were making a great deal of noise, and that this could not be avoided, however much grease was used. We should have to cut through two planks at a distance of about eighteen inches from the ground, but it was becoming clear to us that we should never be able to finish this without being overheard, for it must be remembered that neither the sentry in the courtyard nor the man on the embankment was more than ten yards from us. Our second shock was the discovery that where we lay we were in full view of the parcels-office window. There were always several Germans in this office, which was at the top of the building, and we thought it very probable that we had already been seen. We could not, we said to each other, expect everybody to be blind, and there was a very good chance that the sentry outside would notice the end of our saw. The rain had completely stopped, and we began to realise what an absurdly difficult enterprise we had undertaken. However, there was nothing to be done but push on with the work, though we would not have given much for our chances of success, as things were now. I took off my orderly's clothes and then relieved Baschwitz at his sawing while he did the same. At last the two planks had been cut through, but the wood being wet we had some difficulty in getting them out. We first screwed across them, to hold them together, a piece of wood which we had brought for the purpose, and then, as we prised with our knives, the piece suddenly came away. We replaced it at once, buried the saw and other things that we did not want, closed our knives and put them in our pockets, and then prepared for the worst part of all.

I was to go first, but my position was enviable compared with Baschwitz's, for he would have to replace the plank from outside. I pushed it through, and then, with one arm extended above my head and the other close by my side, I managed after one furious struggle to get through. The first thing I saw was the sentry, but he was standing outside his box with his back towards us and was watching something with great interest in the direction of the river bank. I turned to my left, and crawled up the ditch formed by the paling on one side and the embankment on the other. A few yards ahead of me the ground rose to a level with the railway line, so that beyond this point we should have no means of concealing ourselves. Baschwitz had experienced a certain amount of difficulty in replacing the board, and it must indeed have been a horrible moment for him as he struggled with it. At any moment it might slip and fall with a thud; at any moment the sentry might turn of his own accord, might actually have turned and be aiming now—! But my friend never so much as glanced over his shoulder till he had finished it to his satisfaction. He picked up a handful of mud and rubbed it over the new cut and then crawled slowly towards me, and I patted him on the back, at which he grinned. We reached the point where the ground rose, and having satisfied ourselves that the sentry was not looking in our direction, stood up and—found confronting us, not two yards away, another sentry in charge of some French prisoners working on the line! This man had nothing whatever to do with the camp, but he stared in astonishment at seeing us rise suddenly out of the earth. For one weak moment I felt inclined to duck, but to show that we feared him would have been fatal. I turned, therefore, to Baschwitz and said in German: 'But where can he be? If we've lost that dog there'll be trouble.'

'*Das ist ja wahr,*' he said.

Whistling and peering in all directions, we crossed the line and slid down the embankment on the other side. The camp sentry looked very surprised. No civilian was allowed here, and we had constantly seen even railway officials stopped and questioned. It was obvious that he could not understand how we had got there without his seeing us, but he evidently believed that the other sentry had satisfied himself as to our *bona fides* and had authorised us to pass. We reached the river bank and turned upstream, knowing that from here we could get easily into the town. We scarcely dared to look to right or left, but spoke to each other in German for the benefit of anyone who might pass us. I was glad – my faith, but I was glad, and grateful too, for such luck as we had had comes seldom in a lifetime. As for Baschwitz, this was the first time he had ever succeeded in getting clear of a camp, and he was beside himself. He took me by the arm and squeezed it, 'Honours easy,' he said under his breath, and then aloud:

'*Ich kann es nicht glauben, ich kann es nicht glauben!*' ['I can't believe it, I can't believe it!']

Both men were recaptured. Baschwitz subsequently escaped again, reached England, joined the British Intelligence Service, and returned, by balloon, to organise espionage behind the German lines; he was awarded the D.S.O. Hardy was sent to Fort Zorndorf, where he made three further escape attempts; then to Schweidnitz. In 1918 came his last escape: on 1st March he climbed out of prison and two days later crawled across the Dutch border. His companion, Captain Loder-Symonds [killed soon after], danced in the road in sheer delight, but Hardy simply sat down in the darkness, while the years fell back like a dream. Nothing, he wrote later, would ever equal that moment. He returned to active service in France and was invalided home a few weeks before the Armistice, minus one leg, and with a bullet in his stomach.

9

The Escape of Captain M. C. C. Harrison and Lieutenant H. A. Cartwright from Magdeburg Civil Prison in Germany, 12th May, 1917

Captain Harrison, subsequently Major Harrison, D.S.O., M.C., of The Royal Irish Regiment [and later The Royal Tank Corps], was captured in France on 20th October, 1914; Lieutenant Cartwright, subsequently Captain Cartwright, M.C., of The Duke of Cambridge's Own (The Middlesex Regiment), was captured at Mons on 23rd August, 1914. After the war they wrote an account of their experiences as prisoners of war, taking turn and turn about with the chapters.

The two men met in the prison camp at Burg, made an attempted break together, and were recaptured and separated. Harrison was sent to Torgau, escaped by tunnel, and on recapture, was sent to Magdeburg. Cartwright was sent first to Halle, eventually to Magdeburg, escaped again, and was once more recaptured. In February 1917 they met again in Magdeburg Prison and the partnership was at once resumed. They proposed to escape in disguise and Harrison accordingly began work on transforming his military overcoat.

In due course the alterations to the coat were completed, and as it was still covered with brass buttons and badges of rank, the new roll collar would pass unnoticed provided I wore the garment often enough.

I next had to make arrangements to have it dyed,

since grey mufti overcoats were very uncommon. Although there might be some in existence, the colour would have been sufficiently out of the ordinary to have been conspicuous. Though I had taken the greatest trouble to make every stitch look as if it had been done by machine, and also to press and iron it with my nail, I did not flatter myself that my tailoring was perfect.

Experimenting in my cell with a spare piece of cloth I found it could be dyed a very attractive chocolate colour with a solution of permanganate of potash ($KMNO_4$). I had been allowed some of these crystals as a disinfectant, and as my cell was known to be full of bed bugs, my excessively high demand did not cause special comment. As might be expected, I found, by experiment, that I could get many different shades of chocolate, up to a certain degree of darkness, when the cloth would not take more dye, and no matter how much stronger I made the solution the colour remained the same. This was most satisfactory, as the dyeing process would have to be carried out in my bath when time would be a very important factor.

The bath was in a separate cell on the floor below and each prisoner was locked into it once a week for twenty minutes. It was customary on these occasions to use overcoats for dressing-gowns, and in due course I was marched to the bath cell wearing my newly completed coat (always with brass buttons and badges of rank). Directly I was locked in the cell I let about six inches of water into the bath and then threw in a packet of permanganate crystals. In my endeavour to make a certainty of having a sufficiently strong solution to ensure the garment being dyed the same shade all over, I suppose I must have thrown in about ten times as much permanganate as would have done the job. In a few seconds the coat was a perfect colour all over. I could not leave it

long in the bath knowing the jailer would return in about
ten minutes, and I required at least five to get the water
out of the garment before he came. To my relief I found
that only colourless water came out, so I presumed the
result of this hasty dyeing process would not cause the
coat to dry in patches of different shades of brown.

On removing the plug, to my horror I found I had
also dyed the whole of the bottom of the bath. I hastily
added some more water, as with my soaking overcoat
my only chance now was to get back to my cell before
any suspicion was aroused. Since its arrival in Germany
my coat had had such rough use it is not surprising that
the dirt from it made even this strong solution of permanganate look like genuine filthy water.

Presently the jailer arrived to tell me my time was up.
I was all ready for him with my soaking coat on over my
naked body. Directly he opened the door I ran upstairs
back to my cell, hung the coat up in a corner and put on
some other garments. The jailer, seeing that I had not
emptied the bath proceeded to do so himself. It was not
long before he was after me wanting to know 'what the
hell I had done to the bath?' I told him I had merely
tried to disinfect myself against the vermin in the cell.
Contrary to his usual custom he listened patiently to my
explanation, but terminated the discussion with '*Das ist
ein Schweinerei*'.

A few minutes later I heard him telling the under-
officer of the guard that he was on his way to the Commandant to report 'The filthy habits of the English
captain Harrison'.

A mild storm followed, terminating in my being ordered to pay for a whole new bath.

As the coat dried, my most optimistic hopes were
more than realised. So perfect was the colour, Mr Pullar
might well have been proud had it been dyed at his
works in Perth.

Having nowhere to hide it, I wore it on all possible occasions, which was the best way of averting suspicion.

By the 7th May mobilisation was complete. My cell (No. 20) was not conveniently situated for the contemplated scheme. Cell No. 28 (*page 114*), which would suit me much better, was empty.

How could I persuade the authorities to move me there?

That night as I lay in bed I rubbed the edge of an old bottle against the wall in such a manner as to imitate the sound of a metal file at work. Presently the suspicions of the sentry were aroused, and I could hear the whole guard being warned. I repeated the filing noise at intervals, and suddenly my door was flung open by the under-officer in charge, who found me apparently fast asleep in bed. This was repeated two or three times during the night. The bars in my window were carefully examined the following day. The same performance was continued the next night with a new guard.

On the following day I was moved to cell No. 28.

The moving process is worth recording. It necessitated several journeys, the sentry always following me from one cell to the other with a loaded rifle at full cock pressed against the small of my back. On one of these trips the rifle went off by accident just as I was turning into my cell; the bullet missed me and went into the guard-room, where it caused much havoc but unfortunately hit no one.

The next day I was warned for trials by court martial on 15th May and 18th May. The former was for making a hole in the roof of my cell at Torgau, for which trial I had engaged counsel. The other was for 'insulting superior officers by placing an immoral picture in my cell door'.

Fearing I might be moved to a 'long-sentence' prison

after these trials, we again decided not to wait for them.

Our mobilisation was complete and all that remained to be done was to school the necessary accomplices.

The under-officer in charge of the guard invariably sat at a table by the door of the guard-room, which enabled him to see the length of the corridor, and see that the sentries in the passage never had more than three cell doors open at the same time.

The scheme hinged on this point and required accurate and reliable assistance from two Russian officers and two British, besides temporary inactivity by all the others. Suitable types of sentry and under-officer had to be selected. The guard mounted in the morning, which enabled us to spot beforehand the sentries that would be on duty during the afternoon shifts.

Immediately the orderlies had left the prison, after serving the midday meal, was the time selected. The jailer would be off duty then, so we only had our military guard to contend with.

At 1.45 p.m. on 12th May, 1917 every officer was to be in his cell.

At 1.50 the Russian in cell No. 29 was to knock at his door, and as soon as it was opened would tell the sentry he wanted to get a paper from Loder-Symonds [*see also page 108*] in Cell No. 17. The sentry would go with him to open cell No. 17. As they passed cell No. 25 the Russian inside would knock and ask to go to the lavatory (21). The sentry having now opened two cell doors (29 and 25) would be about to open a third (17).

It was impossible for us to open the cell doors from within, so the Russian from cell No. 25 would have our false key in his possession at this moment. He would go as far as the lavatory and leave that door wide open across the corridor. The doors of cells No. 25 and 29, which were slightly smaller than the lavatory door, would

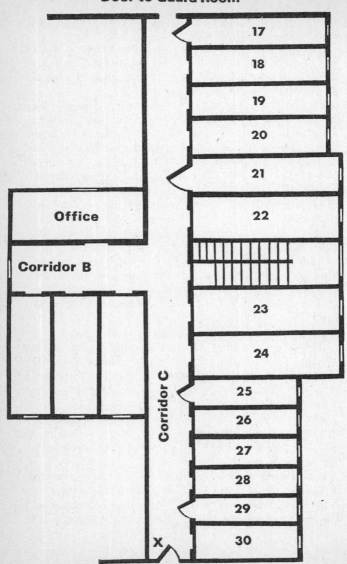

Door to Guard Room

17
18
19
20
21
22

Office

Corridor B

23
24
25
26
27
28
29
30

Corridor C

X

also be left open, thus practically blocking the view along the passage from the guard-room.

As No. 29 and the sentry approached cell 17, No. 25 would rush silently back to Cartwright's cell and open it with the false key, which he would leave in the door and return to the lavatory.

Cartwright would come out of his cell (No. 26), lock it with the false key, bolt it, creep along the passage to my cell (No. 28), let me out, re-lock and re-bolt the door. We would then both proceed quietly to the end of the passage, unbolt and unlock, but not open, Campbell's cell (No. 30) and then open and pass through door X.

As we went out we would hand the key to Campbell, who would relock door X. Loder-Symonds in cell 17 would do all he could to keep the sentry occupied at the door of his cell as long as possible.

No. 25 could lock and bolt Campbell in his cell and hide the key in the passage before returning to his own cell. Ultimately the sentry would lock and bolt cells 17, 25 and 29, which he himself had opened. All other doors would be already locked and bolted, and, what is more, the key would be back in its original hiding place.

It can be readily seen that for the success of this scheme silence and rapidity of action were essentials. Our key being rather smaller than the original required most careful manipulation to ensure this. Further, four accomplices had to be well schooled.

The Russian in cell No. 25 had a very important part to play, and making certain, in a language foreign to both him and us, that he thoroughly understood his part was not easy.

Imagine our feelings as we stood in our cells after the midday meal on 12th May fully dressed, waiting for two Russian officers to set the ball rolling. Of course we had blocked our spy-holes, but had the sentry been inquisitive he might at any moment open our doors to remove the obstruction.

Our watches had been carefully synchronised, and on the stroke of time we heard No. 29 knocking. This was a great relief. No. 25 also knocked at precisely the right moment and in another minute had Cartwright's door open. I next heard my own door being stealthily unlocked and I came out to stand close against the wall beside Cartwright. To my horror I noticed the Russian had not left the lavatory door open, so the view down the passage from the guard-room was only partially blocked by the smaller door of cell No. 25.

We now had to exercise the greatest care in getting round the door of cell 29, which was also open.

I went first and unbolted Campbell's door, leaving Cartwright to relock and bolt mine. As soon as he joined me he unlocked Campbell's door, gave me the key and took up a position of observation at the spy-hole of door 29.

He at once reported all was anything but well and that the sentry was walking back toward us.

Nothing but lightning rapidity could save us. Before I started to tackle door X the sentry must have covered quite half the distance to us. It had evidently been impossible to keep him in conversation at the other end of the passage and he would inevitably have seen us had not Loder-Symonds' last determined effort to entice him back with a bit of food succeeded. As Campbell took the key we walked boldly out. A woman was cleaning the steps on the other side of the door, so, on the spur of the moment, I said 'Malzeit' [*meal-time*] over my shoulder, as if speaking to the sentry who had let us out, and we proceeded down the stairs, through the municipal building and out into the street.

Before proceeding further it might be as well to narrate

the events that occurred in the prison immediately after our departure.

It will be remembered that the adventure started at 1.50, and, interminable as it may have seemed at the time, I don't suppose it was more than three minutes from then before we were through door X.

Campbell shut this door after us, but had not time to lock it.

When the sentry locked the Russian back in cell No. 28 he noticed Campbell's door was unlocked. He just looked in, saw Campbell was inside and locked and bolted it then and there, possibly thinking it might not have been properly shut after the midday meal. At 2 p.m. the sentries were relieved and the new man noticing door X was unlocked, opened it, looked out and was seen by the woman, and promptly locked it.

A few minutes later a police sergeant arrived to report that some silly woman had told him that two officers had just escaped. Evidently the charwoman on the stairs had recognised me, as I had passed her several times on my visits to the dentist. The under-officer in charge of the guard was at once woken up, much to his annoyance, and he at once pointed to his row of locked cell doors and told the police sergeant to go away and mind his own business.

Later it was given out that the second sentry was held responsible for our escape and was shot. Whether this was true or whether the man was merely sent elsewhere I cannot say, but it was firmly believed by all subsequent guards.

By 2.5 p.m. all was quiet again and nothing unusual happened till 2.40, when Captain Kunz arrived to inform me that I was to pay three hundred and fifty marks for damage to Government property in Torgau. All efforts to open my cell door failed until a locksmith had been called in, when the door was thrown open to an

117

empty cell. (From previous experience we had discovered that unless the greatest care was used when manipulating our key, the lock was left in such a position that the proper key could not be made to function afterwards.)

When Captain Kunz had recovered from his first shock he suggested that I must be in Captain Cartwright's cell, and orders were sent to go and see. A further struggle with the lock resulted in the door being flung open ten minutes later to another empty cell.

Captain Kunz's strong point was not an ability to control his temper, and he now gave one of the finest exhibitions imaginable.

He shouted at everybody he could see and ordered all the other cell doors to be opened. He stampeded up and down the passage checking each prisoner himself about half a dozen times in an effort to identify Cartwright and me, and when he had done cursing all the guard he got busy on the telephone. A further invasion by the camp Commandant's staff took place in about ten minutes' time.

The key by now had been restored to its hiding-place in the passage, where it survived all subsequent searches.

Cartwright and Harrison were recaptured twelve nights later and separated. Harrison was sent to Ströhen; escaped on 20th August, 1917, crossed the Dutch frontier early on the morning of 4th September, and returned to England, rejoining his regiment in France that December. Cartwright followed some eleven months later, climbing out of prison in Aachen on 4th August, 1918. Home in England, Harrison, who had been wounded and sent on leave, was best man at Cartwright's marriage. 'We gave a special thought to our mutual friend, the Commandant at Magdeburg, and sent him a wedding photograph—suitably inscribed!'

10

The Attempts of
Oberleutnant H. H. E. Justus to escape
from imprisonment in England, 1917–1918

*Oberleutnant Heinz Justus of the Hanoverian Fusiliers was
taken prisoner at Langemark by the Irish Guards on 31st July,
1917, and sent to imprisonment in England.*

The first English camp I was taken to as a German
prisoner of war in July 1917 was Colsterdale, near
Masham, up north in Yorkshire, and I hope it will be
taken in good part when I say that I didn't want to stay
there. I tried several times to get through the barbed
wire and I also took part in one of the tunnelling schemes
which was, however, discovered by the British just before
the tunnel was completed. Then one fine day I hit upon
the idea of just walking out through the gate disguised
as our English canteen manager, who was about my
size and figure – his name was Mr Budd – I wonder if,
by chance, he may read these words and if he still re-
members it all. So evening after evening I started observing closely his every movement on leaving the camp, and
noticed to my satisfaction that the sentries never asked
him for the password. Everybody knew Mr Budd too
well for that. This was also, of course, rather a drawback;
but my idea was to do the thing in the evening after dark.
   I'd been informed – I think quite wrongly – that every

male passenger in those war days was supposed to produce a pass or other document when booking a railway
ticket, particularly when travelling to London, and as I
didn't feel like walking the whole way there I decided to
travel as a woman.

We had private codes between the camps and our
people at home so I sent a message to my mother asking
her to send me every conceivable thing which I should
need for this disguise. After some time I received news
that a wig was arriving camouflaged as tobacco; that all
sorts of fake jewellery, a compass and similar handy
things had been sent off in marmalade jars, or baked in a
cake – and, last but not least, that I would soon receive a
large quilt with a skirt, petticoat, veil, some sort of a hat,
silk stockings and a nice silk coat all sewn up in it. I had
asked for everything in black, even the necklace and
brooches, as I wanted to look like a poor widow so that
people on the trains wouldn't speak to me as freely as if I
were dressed as a giddy young girl.

Then I heard rumours of Mr Budd being transferred
to some other camp, so I couldn't afford to wait for the
arrival of these mysterious packages and began collecting
an outfit in the camp. My skirt was made out of an old
blanket and the hat and muff were mostly composed of
parts of fur waistcoats. We had plenty of fancy costumes
in the camp, beautiful wigs, hats, and so on, but they
were all under 'word of honour' not to be used except
for theatrical purposes, and so of course I couldn't use
them.

Then the great day arrived and I put on all the clothes,
man and woman's mixed together, so that I was able to
change from one to the other with a few slight manipula-
tions.

I approached the gate disguised as Mr Budd with a
false moustache and a pair of spectacles, worn exactly
the way Mr Budd wore them. My cap, mackintosh and

bag were also exact replicas of the ones with which Mr Budd used to leave the camp every evening. Even the most pessimistic of my friends thought I really was Mr Budd when they saw me.

Mr Budd was in the habit of leaving the camp about 8 p.m. and I had timed my attempt for about ten minutes to eight. Meanwhile a few friends of mine would keep the real Mr Budd busy in the canteen until shortly *after* eight, and as the sentries were usually changed at 8 o'clock sharp I was sure that the new sentry would not be surprised to see the second and real Mr Budd leaving camp. So off I went straight to the gate gaily smoking my pipe as if after a good day's work at the canteen. A few yards from it I shouted 'Guard,' as this was the way Mr Budd used to announce himself day by day. The sentry called out, 'Who's there?' 'Budd,' I answered. 'Right,' he said and opened the big door.

I walked slowly down the street from the camp towards Masham station. I had about a two-hours' walk before me; but I hadn't gone more than fifty yards when I espied our Commandant coming towards me. Within a fraction of a second I had torn off the moustache and spectacles as, of course, I didn't want the Colonel to address the false Mr Budd. As I passed him I just said 'Good evening,' and so did he.

A little further on I decided to change into a woman. This was only a matter of a few seconds. I exchanged Mr Budd's cap with the woman's hat and veil which I carried in my bag, and took off my mackintosh, which covered a navy-blue civilian jacket, trimmed with all sorts of lace and bows. My skirt was hitched up with a leather belt round my hips so I had only to undo the belt to release the skirt. Luckily for me skirts in those days reached down to the ground, so my leggings were completely covered by the skirt and couldn't be seen in the dark.

I met some Tommies on the road, and they all behaved very decently; they all bade me 'good evening', and none of them insisted on starting a conversation with the very reserved woman who did not even reply to their 'good evening'.

Only once I was a bit troubled, by a shepherd's dog, but he soon withdrew when the strange woman took something out of her muff and sprinkled it on the road. It is very important for an escaper always to carry a box of pepper to defend himself against dogs.

I'd been walking now for quite some time, making good progress towards the station of Masham, when I noticed three soldiers following me and overtaking me. One of them was equipped with a rifle with fixed bayonet and I knew that this must surely be a sentry from the camp as there were no other military in the neighbourhood. I at once thought of throwing away my bag which might so easily give me away, but anything of that sort would immediately have aroused suspicion. The soldiers came steadily closer and closer until finally they overtook me. They then stopped and said 'Good evening, miss. Have you by any chance seen a man with a bag like yours? A prisoner of war has escaped and we are out looking for him.' Well, I tried for a time, really only for a very short time, to speak in a high voice, telling them please not to bother a decent young girl by starting a conversation with her, but all they said was might they have a look at the bag I carried. I refused, of course, but it was only a matter of another few seconds before I realised that it was all over with me. I was found out. I then learned that my escape had been discovered owing to the sentry not being released as usual at 8 o'clock. So you can easily understand that a mysterious situation occurred when shortly after 8 o'clock a second Mr Budd appeared and asked the same sentry to be let through the gate. The ensuing confusion was quite amusing, of

course, and the bell was immediately rung, but unfortunately I hadn't heard it.

Well, there was nothing for it but to be escorted back
to the camp. One Tommy carried my bag, which was
not, however, due to gallantry on his part towards a lady,
but mainly because he feared I might throw it into the
small river we had to cross. I would, however, not have
thrown it away as a good deal of my money was in it,
which later in the same evening was returned to me by
the British, as they never suspected that the small package of Gillette blades did not contain razor blades but
six English pound notes folded to exactly the size of a
safety razor blade wrapped up in the original Gillette
paper and envelope.

There was, of course, a great excitement amongst the
British officers. The Commandant, the Assistant Commandant, the Adjutant and several other officers had all
assembled in the guardroom anxiously awaiting news of
the escaped officer, and you cannot possibly imagine the
funny faces they made when the door was opened by my
escort and in walked a woman wearing a white fur hat.
I think the first thing that happened was that everybody
burst out laughing. Then the Commandant said that it
was not at all customary for a young lady to undress in
the presence of so many gentlemen, but that in this particular case an exception to the rule must be made. I
could not, however, undo the knot of my petticoat tape,
which my friends had tied too tight. I therefore asked if
perhaps one of the gentlemen would be kind enough
to help undo the thing, and the Adjutant very kindly
drew forth his pocket knife, which finally settled the
question.

*Justus was court-martialled and sentenced to 35 days. He was
then sent to Holyport, near Maidenhead, where he made two
attempts to crawl out through the barbed wire. The authorities*

decided to transfer him to Wakefield with fifty other officers. He made up his mind to break from the train on the journey north.

I passed the next few hours in a rather nervous and excited state. It was about a quarter to six when, after a short stop, we left the station of South Elmshall. The train moved very slowly but was speeding up every second – there were fields on both sides of the track, and as it was sufficiently dark already it was quite clear to me that the time had come to do the trick. My fellow officers were, of course, very much surprised when I asked them all of a sudden to stand up right away and place themselves before the door and the windows of the corridor so that the sentry would not be able to see me jumping out of the window. They were sporting enough to do exactly what I asked of them, and a few seconds later I found myself on a meadow by the side of the track. The tail lights of the train disappeared into the dark and I was free, absolutely free – nobody who hasn't been a prisoner can possibly imagine what this really means.

The first thing to do now was to put on my civilian cap and I then turned down the collar of my tunic. The German officers' uniforms are so made that the collar fits high round the neck, so in order to hide the German tunic collar I had to roll it down – and as I wasn't in possession of a white collar and a tie I just wound a handkerchief round the neck. This didn't look so very smart but it served the purpose.

I now walked the short distance back to South Elmshall and proceeded to Doncaster, whence I wanted to take a train up to London. My general scheme was eventually to go to some seaport on the west coast, and to smuggle on board some neutral ship, preferably a Spanish one, as I had learnt that language in the camps. I had decided on Cardiff but I thought I would go to London first because it would certainly be easier for the

The Escape of H. H. E. Justus

first few days to hide in a big city than in a small place.

I arrived in Doncaster at about a quarter past seven in the evening, and found out that there was no train to London before 4.50 or so, I think it was, in the morning. Well, this was really a nuisance, but all I could do was to just make the best of a bad business, and I started out from the station to have a look round the town. There were big signposts advertising a show with the name of 'You Are Spotted', which was indeed a rather apposite title for a play from the point of view of an escaped prisoner. I decided to have a look at it. At about half-past eight I made for the theatre, which I deliberately entered a little late because I preferred to take my seat only after the lights in the auditorium had been turned out, as I couldn't even take off my rain-coat, and I had no collar. So when I came in, the show was already in full swing and I was greeted from the stage by a chorus of about twenty or thirty girls waving Allied flags and singing the most exciting rag-times. I can hardly describe my sensations at all this. About three hours ago I was still a prisoner of war, and I couldn't help smiling when I noticed that my neighbour to the right was an English Staff Officer. When the lights went on after the first act he looked at me a little longer than I liked at the moment, and then I heard him say to his companion that I was rather a strange-looking fellow. But that was all, and nobody kept me from enjoying the rest of the show more than anybody else in the house. When the thing was over the band of course played 'God Save the King', and I wondered what my neighbours would have said if I had joined in and sung the German words to it, as we have the same tune for a German patriotic song.

Finally the time arrived for me to go to the station. They didn't ask for passes or anything, and I soon had my ticket, and at about 9 o'clock in the morning I arrived at King's Cross, the station which I had left the day before under rather different circumstances. The first thing to do was to buy a good collar and tie, and also a waistcoat to put over my tunic, I then started out for a nice walk through London. Trafalgar Square was one of the few places I remembered from a short visit I paid to this country as a boy in pre-war days, but I was very much surprised indeed to find that it all looked different now. Trafalgar Square in those days was turned into a devastated French village, probably for some Red Cross collection or a similar purpose; there were trenches, shattered houses, barbed wire, shell holes, guns and all that, all of which I inspected with the eye of an expert. I then strolled down the Strand, and after a while I went to the matinee of a show called 'Going Up', at the Gaiety Theatre. I have seen a good many shows since 1918 but I do not think I saw a better one than this 'Going Up'.

After this experience I again wandered around the streets of London, had supper at some small restaurant and then began to think about where to go for the night. I passed a man in the street who looked rather a rough and the right sort of fellow probably to ask for some information of this kind, so I offered him a cigarette and started a conversation. I told him that I was in London for the first time and could he suggest some convenient lodgings for the night where they would not ask for passes, as sometimes you didn't exactly want to give your real name.

He gave me the tip to go to some small hotel near one of the big stations where they probably wouldn't be so very strict, but still he wasn't quite sure if I wouldn't be asked to show papers there, too. I told him that I had been to the Gaiety in the afternoon, and speaking of theatres he said that I should by all means go and see the extraordinarily fine play, 'The Hidden Hand', at the Middlesex Theatre. It was awfully good, about the war

and the Germans and spying and all that. I said I would
certainly go, and I did. It was the third time that I had
been in a theatre within twenty-four hours, and I very
soon realised that this was a very, very thrilling play indeed. But after a while I came to think that it was a little
too thrilling perhaps for a man in German uniform, even
if his military attire was covered by a rain-coat. It was
the most anti-German performance in the world, and
the whole atmosphere around me didn't seem to be very
pro-German. I really wondered what would happen if
by some chance or other somebody would find out that
there was a German officer right in their midst – they
would probably have torn me to pieces, and when the
lights were switched on after the first act everybody
seemed to look at me in a very suspicious way. All of
them, just a few seconds ago, had been told from the stage
all about German spies and all sorts of nice things about
the nice Germans. I fancied I could hear them whisper to
one another, 'Do you see that funny chap in a mackintosh? Everybody has taken off his coat, why hasn't he?
Well, as a matter of fact, nobody of course said such
things, but after all I thought it might be just as safe to
leave the house after the first act, which had given me
already a complete run for my money. When I went down
the stairs I tried to look just as 'Allied' as possible and I
remember quite distinctly that I whistled the Marseil-
laise in order to be taken for a Frenchman, or at least for
a man with strongly anti-German feelings.

It was about time now to think of going to a hotel. If
after all they asked for a passport or something I would
just say I'd lost mine and the only consequence would
probably be that they wouldn't give me a room. But at
all events they would be desirous to know my name, and
so I decided to adopt for the night the name of Albert
Georges, which could be either French or English, and I
thought it might be a good idea to perhaps say that I was

a Frenchman if they asked too many uncomfortable questions. The first two or three hotels were full up, but in the next one they said, 'Yes, there was a small room, and would I please fill in this form here.' Very well, then, my name was Albert Georges, last address: Southampton. Street? Well, I hadn't thought of that, but I think I wrote Queen Street, hoping that this would be the name of a street in Southampton. Nationality: French. 'Oh, you are a Frenchman,' the young lady at the hotel said. 'There are special forms for foreigners,' and so she handed me a great big piece of paper with innumerable questions to be answered. Not only did they want to know absolutely everything about myself, but they wanted to know also all about my parents, and where my grandfather had been born and a thousand questions of that sort. I became quite dizzy and all the time, in order to think of some new name or date, I pretended I couldn't very well write with those extraordinary nibs; in France, of course, we had quite different nibs and all that. Finally I got through with it. I was never asked for a passport, and I smiled when I was shown into my room. But when I was in bed I became uneasy; had I said King Street or was it Queen Street, and what was the number of the house I had given, and what did I say was my great-grandfather's uncle's first name, and what age had I given? Imagine the consequences if for some unforeseen reason or other they asked me again for one of the many dates and names I had given, and if I didn't remember then the date of my own birthday or something. Well, I switched on the lights again and wrote down on a piece of paper whatever I remembered of all the many dates and names I had given, but I was glad that nobody came to compare my present notes with the ones I had given downstairs.

I had a *very* good night's rest, and felt fine and cheerful when I left the hotel next morning. There was a Red Cross day on or something, and soon I was stopped in the street by a kind elderly lady who insisted on selling me a little Union Jack which she tried to pin on to my mackintosh. However, the pin wouldn't go through and the trouble was that she always stabbed against the Iron Cross which I was wearing on my tunic. I thought of telling her I was sorry to say that at the moment the Union Jack didn't go so very well with the Iron Cross, but I didn't. I just took the flag out of her hand and fastened it myself on a spot just above my decoration.

I now wanted to get rid of my tunic at the earliest possible moment. I had already thought of throwing the thing into the Thames, but it was a brand new one and it was quite probable after all that one of these days I would find myself back again in a prison camp, where I would miss the nice uniform very much. So I decided just to send the tunic by parcel post to the Commandant of my old camp, Holyport, as I wasn't sure about the exact address of the new camp near Wakefield. I suppose that the Holyport Commandant was much surprised to receive that parcel. I read a few days later in all the papers that he had got it all right.

I now proceeded to buy a pair of trousers and a jacket, and at last I looked like a real civilian and I was now able to take off my mackintosh.

The following night I again tried to register as a Frenchman. I went of course to another hotel, but the young lady there said that no foreigners could be admitted before they had registered at the police station. She told me where the police station was, and I promised to be back in a few minutes – but of course I never returned. I just became an Englishman and spent the night at one of those small hotels near Waterloo Station.

There was much influenza in England in those days,

and when I woke up next morning I didn't feel very well, but still I didn't pay any attention to that, and I decided to go to Cardiff in the evening. I was still in possession of a nice sum of money to carry on for quite some time, including a bribe or two to help me to get on a Spanish ship in Cardiff, but I thought it might be good to get some more funds before leaving London, so I decided to sell a valuable platinum and diamond ring I was wearing. My mother had given it to me as a talisman for the trenches, and as I didn't much care for such a showy thing I had accepted it on the clear understanding that I could sell it again once it had done its good work at the front. So I went to offer it at a jeweller's shop, in Fleet Street I think it was, and said I wanted fifty guineas for it. The man said that it was really a very fine ring, but would I produce some proof or something in order to show where it came from. I said my father had given it to me the last time we were in Paris. 'Oh, yes,' of course he didn't doubt a bit that everything was perfectly in order, and quite all right, but you see these days now you had to be very careful buying things like that – and finally he asked if he might have a look at my registration card or something of that sort which I had never heard of before in my life. I said yes, certainly, but after going through all my pockets I said that I must have left the thing at my hotel and I would go and get it. Everything seemed to be quite all right except that the man didn't seem to care about returning the ring to me. He *knew* that there was something wrong, and he disappeared once more to talk the matter over with another man in the back of the shop. For a second or so I thought of just dashing out of the place, but then the man came out again and said, 'I'll give you seventeen guineas.' I protested, of course, but both of us very quickly realised that it must be either yes or no, and so I accepted, and then beat it just as fast as possible. The only thing I failed to understand was why on earth he had offered me *seventeen* guineas; I would just as soon have accepted seventeen shillings.

I now went to Cardiff by train, arrived about 9 p.m., and went to the Royal Hotel. I gave my name as Allan Hinckley, who was an American opera singer in pre-war days in Hamburg. I told the porter right away that I had my luggage at the station, and if anybody had asked me for a passport or something I would just have said that I had that in my suitcase. After having written my name in the hotel book I asked if they could send some-body to the station to get my luggage, but I said this, of course, only for show, as I really didn't have any luggage at all, and when the porter said of course he could send for it, I said, 'Well, I think after all I'll leave it just where it is; I've got to go back to London anyhow early in the morning, and I'd like to turn in right away.'

I felt very miserable when I awoke next morning, and I was quite sure now that I had the real 'flu, but I set out in order to see if I could spot a Spanish ship somewhere. I had no idea where the port was and somebody told me that there was a place of the name of Penarth, which was right on the open sea. I went there in a taxi, but was awfully disappointed to find a deserted pleasure resort with no ships whatsoever leaving there for Spain. I went to a small hotel and had a whisky and soda in the de-serted lounge. I sat quite by myself by the fireside, and read various articles which had been published in the Press about my escape. One paper had a big headline: 'Masquerading Hun Officer in Woman's Dress.' Appar-ently Scotland Yard thought I was doing the same thing again. While I was reading this a British officer came in, accompanied by two ladies. They all sat down quite close to me in order to get warm at the same fire, and im-mediately started talking about the war.

The officer had just come from France on short leave,

and one of the girls said rather embarrassing things about the Germans – I mean embarrassing for a German officer who sat impersonating a harmless civilian in the same room. She said these Germans must be really frightful people and she was sure that they all were the greatest cowards in the world, and many other delightful things. The British officer, however, had a rather different opinion. He said that he hadn't noticed that the Germans were cowards; he had just come from the Western Front, where he had been stationed opposite a Prussian Guards division, and he had a great respect for them. Well, I tell you, when this officer spoke I very nearly butted in. I felt like saying to him, 'Now, look here, I'm a German officer myself, let's talk things over for an hour or so, and we can toss for drinks anyhow. Later on, of course, you must hand me over to the police, but that cannot be helped and I don't want to miss this opportunity of comparing notes with a decent fellow from the other side of "No Man's Land".'

But I did nothing of the kind as it would have been the immediate and abrupt end of my escapade and I had still faint hopes of getting away to Spain some time and somehow.

My Penarth excursion had not improved my health at all, and I felt very, very miserable indeed when I was back once more in Cardiff. I went to another hotel that night, the Queen's, where I registered under the name of Henry Hughes, and I told the people there exactly the same story about my luggage. Everything went quite all right except my health, as I was very sick indeed next morning. My temperature had gone up in an alarming way and I felt absolutely run down. But I carried on for another day. I went back that night again to the hotel, and the porter was much surprised to see me again, but I had given very liberal tips in the morning and everybody was very kind to me; the whole staff knew already that the so-called Mr Henry Hughes was very much under the weather.

The following day was one of the darkest in my prisoner-of-war history. I felt so ill that I was at last obliged to go to the police station and give myself up; I was too sick a man to carry on with my plans, which after all required perfect health and perfect nerves.

I was sent back next day to the new camp, Lofthouse Park, near Wakefield, where I got the right medical treatment, and when I had recovered there was the usual court martial and the subsequent 'vacation' at good old Chelmsford prison. I got fifty-six days this time; and my tunic, which I had sent to the Commandant at Holyport, was returned to me here, in perfect condition.

Justus spent Christmas 1918 in Chelmsford Prison. He was sent back to Germany in July, 1919.

II

*The Escape of Captains Johnston, Yearsley,
Ellis, Haig, Grant, Clarke and Harris, and
Lieutenant-Commander Cochrane, R.N., from
Yozgad P.O.W. Camp in Turkey to the
island of Cyprus, a distance of four hundred
and fifty miles, 7th August to 12th
September, 1918*

*On the night of 7th August, 1918, a party of eight officers broke
out of Yozgad P.O.W. Camp in Turkey: Captain M. A. B.
Johnston of the Royal Regiment of Artillery (Royal Garrison
Artillery), Captain K. D. Yearsley of the Royal Engineers,
Captain A. B. Haig of the 24th Punjabis, Captain V. S. Clarke
of the Royal West Kent Regiment, Captain J. H. Harris of the
Hampshire Regiment (all five were subsequently awarded the
M.C.), Captain R. A. P. Grant, M.C., of the 112th Infantry,
Captain F. R. Ellis of the Duke of Cornwall's Light Infantry,
and Lieutenant-Commander A. D. Cochrane, D.S.O., R.N.
(subsequently promoted to Commander), a submarine officer.*

*Under Cochrane's leadership, they headed south across Turkey
towards the Mediterranean coast. Two weeks later, still free,
they were struggling across the Anatolian Plateau towards the
Taurus Mountains.*

[*20th August*] By this time our throats were parched with
thirst and our clothes saturated with perspiration; but

worst discomfort of all was the pain of our feet. The violent running and marching, the fiery heat of the sun above, and the radiation from the glowing earth beneath, had combined to reduce them to bits of red-hot flesh, and we longed for water to cool them. But everywhere stretched the desert, dusty and bare, bordered by naked barren hills. To avoid approaching those immediately S. of us, we had latterly altered our course rather to the S.E.; for we were developing an unholy and not unnatural dread of brigands, and imagined that every hill was infested with them.

Not till 4.30 that evening did we dare to take more than a few minutes' rest. As we lay on the ground we scrutinised with deepest interest the Taurus Mountains, which, as the heat-haze lifted, stood out clearly ahead – the last great barrier to be overcome before we reached the sea. From a distance of about sixty miles it looked a level range, broken by no outstanding peak, pierced by no low-lying pass. Anywhere in the portion where we were likely to cross, however, the map indicated a height of not more than 5000 feet; so we turned our attention to nearer objects. In the next shallow valley we could see several flocks of sheep, or so we thought. These we watched eagerly through our glasses, for their presence denoted water. We fancied we could see a stream a little beyond them, but when we reached the spot after dark we found that mirage had once again deceived us. It was not until we had marched another sixteen weary miles that our needs were to be met.

That night, the beginning of our third week of liberty, the strain of recent events and our anxiety for water were reflected in our tempers, and Cochrane had the thankless task of trying to keep the balance between those who demanded water on or off the nearest route, and those who howled for smooth-going for the sake of their agonised feet. A twentieth-century Solomon, he kept the balance well: for the sore-feet brigade he had two hours over an ideal marching surface; then, in deference to the all-for-water party, two hours over stone-strewn ground at the foot of some low hills. These held out the best prospect of finding the precious fluid. The search, however, was all in vain; for although we passed close above a village where there must have been water, we did not dare to seek the source of its supply. This night opium pills and 'Kola' tablets were in great demand, but even those could not keep some of us going, and soon after midnight we took an hour's rest. A little before, we had passed by an enormous flock of sheep: so disheartened were some of us that we very nearly decided to go up and ask the shepherd to show us the nearest water. This, however, Cochrane wisely decided not to risk. Instead, while the remainder lay down and rested, he left his pack and went off with Old Man [*Haig*] to search for it.

Their self-sacrifice was without result. After an hour's absence they rejoined the party, and we marched on, determined to make a last desperate effort to reach the Ak Gueul (White Lake) near Eregli. This was still fifteen miles or more away, and would, we knew, be salt; but it was the next water marked on our map.

[*21st August*] Late that afternoon the sun appeared for a time, enabling most of us to snatch a little sleep. This was what was needed more than anything else. Much refreshed, we left our rude shelter at 6 p.m., and hurriedly refilling our water-bottles at the well, continued across the valley. Within an hour we were lying at the top of the low ridge on its southern side. From here we overlooked the bare plain stretching to the marshes near Eregli, and thought we saw the reflection of water in the Ak Gueul. When six hours later, and after covering seventeen or eighteen miles, we reached the lake, it was to find that it was dry, and that it had been only the white salt-

crusted basin that we had seen. There was nothing to do
but carry on. Besides the need of water to keep us moving,
an icy wind blew without respite upon our backs, making
even the short hourly halts a misery. Secondly, we had on
the previous day checked our food supply, and calculated
we had only enough for another four days at the most.
Meanwhile, there still remained the Taurus range to be
crossed.

*On 30th August, twenty-three nights after their break-out, they
reached the sea, having marched clear across the Taurus Mountains: 330 miles behind them, 120 miles to go. The sea was
bright, still as glass, and empty. They camped in a ravine full of
flies, and lived on an abandoned store of dirty wheat, ground in
an old coffee grinder, and muddy water. By the 35th day they
were depressed, almost apathetic. It was then that a motorboat
sailed into view, flying the Turkish and German flags, towing a
lighter and a dinghy, and anchored in the creek. After moonset
Cochrane, Grant, Haig and Clarke set off on 'the last great
venture' to try to bribe her crew.*

The others moved all the kit close down to the edge of
the rock where a boat could come in.

An anxious wait ensued. The four had set out at
9 o'clock, but it was not till 11.30 that Looney [*Yearsley*],
with his last reserve – half a biscuit – gone, saw a boat
coming silently towards him. In a trice the other three
were awakened. Was it friend or foe? She had four men
on board: they were our four. The moment the boat
touched at the rock the kit was thrown in. Cochrane had
done magnificent work. He had swum round the creek,
found out that there was no one in the motor-boat, cut
away the dinghy belonging to the lighter, swum back
with it, and fetched the other three.

Eight hopeful fugitives were soon gently paddling the
dinghy towards the creek, keeping, so far as might be, in

the shadow of the cliffs; for though the moon was down, the stars seemed to make the open bay unpleasantly light. As noiselessly as possible the dinghy came alongside the motor-boat and made fast. The creek here was about sixty yards wide. The tug, moored by a heavy chain and anchor, was in the middle of it. Some fifteen yards away was the lighter; on this were several men, one of whom was coughing the whole time we were 'cutting out' the motor-boat. This took us a full hour.

On trying the weight of the chain and anchor, Cochrane decided to loose the motor-boat from her anchorage by dropping the chain overboard. He did not think it would be possible to weigh the anchor. Odd lengths of cord were collected and joined up in readiness for lowering the end of the chain silently when the time came. But success was not to be attained so easily. Boarding the motor-boat, Nobby and Perce [*Clarke and Harris*] had, foot by foot, got rid of almost all the chain which lay in the bows, when another score of fathoms were discovered below deck. It would be quicker, after all, to weigh anchor, and by superhuman efforts this was at length achieved without attracting the attention of the enemy, our coats and shirts being used as padding over the gunwale.

As soon as the anchor was weighed, we connected the motor-boat with the dinghy by a tow-rope found on the former; all got back into the dinghy, and in this we paddled quietly away. With our home-made paddles and heavy tow we were unable to make much headway. With six paddles in the water, we could credit ourselves with a speed of not so much as a single knot.

Once clear of the bay, Cochrane again went aboard the motor-boat and this time had a look at the engine. We had remaining at this time about an inch of candle, but this served a very useful purpose. By its glimmer Cochrane was able to discover and light a hurricane-lamp. He told us the joyous news that there was a fair quantity of paraffin in the tank. Unfortunately no petrol was to be found, and it seemed unlikely that we should be able to start the engine from cold on paraffin alone. So weak indeed were we, that it was all we could do to turn over the engine at all. While frantic efforts were being made by Cochrane and Nobby to start her, those in the dinghy continued paddling. After three hours all were very tired of it, and very grateful for a slight off-shore breeze which gave us the chance of setting a sail. Cochrane rigged up our main-sail on the motor-boat; all then clambered aboard the latter.

Our speed was now quite good and many times that of our most furious paddling. Suddenly looking back, we saw the dinghy adrift and disappearing in the darkness behind us. Whoever had been holding the rope at the dinghy end had omitted to make fast on coming on board the motor-boat. The dinghy still contained all our kit; so to recover this, including as it did what food and water remained to us, Cochrane and Johnny [*Johnston*] jumped overboard and swam back to it. The sail on the motor-boat had been furled, and in a few minutes the dinghy was again in tow.

After this slight misadventure the engine-room was once more invaded, and Looney and Cochrane experimented with the magneto. There was a loose wire and vacant terminal which they were uncertain whether to connect or not. Eventually, with Nobby turning over the engine, a shock was obtained with the two disconnected. Two were now put on to the starting-handle. But the cramped space produced several bruised heads and nothing else as pair after pair struggled on.

At length at 4.30 a.m., little more than an hour before dawn, the engine started up with a roar, in went the clutch, and off went the motor-boat at a good seven knots. At the time when the engine began firing, Nobby, who was feeling much the worse for his exertions in weighing anchor followed by his efforts to start the motor, was lying on deck in the stern. Startled by the sudden series of explosions, he thought for a moment that a machine-gun had opened fire at short range, till he discovered that he was lying on the exhaust-pipe, the end of which was led up on deck!

We reckoned that by this time we were some three miles from the creek, so we could hope that the roar of the engine would be inaudible to those on shore. On the other hand, sunrise on the 12th September was a little before 6 a.m., so that dawn should have found us still within view from the land. A kindly mist, however, came down and hid us till we were well out to sea. As soon as it was light enough we tried to declutch in order to transfer our kit from the dinghy to the tug. But the clutch was in bad order and would not come out. The alternative was to haul up the dinghy level with the tug, with the motor still running, and then to transfer all our goods and chattels on to the deck. It was a difficult task, but it was done. We then turned the dinghy adrift. This meant the gain of an additional two knots.

It now seemed as if our troubles really were nearing their end. The engine was running splendidly, the main tank was full to the brim; there was enough and to spare of lubricating oil, and in a barrel lashed to the deck in the stern was found some more paraffin. A beaker contained sufficient water to give us each a mugful. It was brackish, but nectar compared to the well-water which we had been drinking for the last fortnight. We also allowed ourselves some chupatties and a handful of raisins.

Our principal fear now was of being chased by one of the seaplanes which we thought to be stationed at Mersina, not many miles away. We had seen one on two occasions during our stay in the ravine. Time went on,

however, and nothing appeared. Instead of looking behind us for a seaplane we began to look ahead, hoping
to come across one of our own patrol boats. It says much
for the deserted condition of those waters that during our
fortnight on the coast and our voyage of about 120 miles
to Cyprus not a single boat was seen save those that we
had seen in the creek.

Discussing the matter of the discovery of the loss of the
motor-boat and the subsequent action of the crew, we
came to the cheerful conclusion that probably the loss
would not be divulged to the authorities for a considerable period. The rightful crew would know what to expect
as a punishment for their carelessness, and would either
perjure themselves by swearing that the boats had sunk
at their moorings, or thinking discretion even better than
perjury, disappear into the deserted hinterland through
which we had marched. Should these two guesses be
wrong, there was yet another course which we thought
possible, though not so probable, for the crew to take.
Thinking that the motor-boat and dinghy had drifted
away, they would not mention their disappearance till
a thorough search had been made of all bays and creeks
within a few miles of the locality.

The cherry of this delightful cocktail of fancy was very
palatable; whatever else happened, the occupants of the
lighter, agitated to the extreme and dinghyless, would
have to swim ashore, and this thought amused us greatly.

Till noon the sea was sufficiently rough to be breaking
continually over the bows, and three of the party were
feeling the effect of the roll. To the rest, to be thus rocked
in the cradle of the deep, borne ever nearer to freedom,
was a sensation never to be forgotten. The motor was
going splendidly, and we all took turns at the wheel,
steering by the 'sun-compass', and, with the exception of
Cochrane, very badly.

By 1.30 p.m. we could recognise the dim outline of the high mountain-range of Cyprus: on the strength of this we each ate another two chupatties and a handful of raisins, finishing our meal with a quarter of a mugful of water.

But we were a trifle premature in our lavishness. Our troubles were not at an end, for half an hour later the engine began to fail, and, while Cochrane was below looking for the cause of the trouble, she petered out. The fault was subsequently traced to the over-heating of one of the main shaft bearings, the oil feed-pipe to which had been previously broken, and had vibrated from its place. Having satisfied himself that no serious damage was done, Cochrane decided to wait half an hour for the bearing to cool.

When the bearing had cooled, we tried to start the engine again. One pair followed another on the starting-handle, but all to no purpose. All four sparking-plugs were examined: the feed-pipe, separator, and carburetter were taken down. Except for a little water in the separator, all seemed correct. We refilled the tank with paraffin from the barrel on deck, but our renewed attempts still met with no success. Our efforts to turn the crank became more and more feeble, until, by 4.30 p.m., we lay down on deck utterly exhausted.

Just before sunset we decided we would make a final attempt to start up. Should that be unsuccessful, we would set the sails; but to our great relief she fired at the second attempt. Our joy was somewhat tempered by her refusing to run for more than a few minutes at a time. It was found that this was caused by the feed-pipe from the tank repeatedly choking, owing, no doubt, to grit in the oil obtained from the barrel, which, as we had noticed when pouring it in, was very dirty.

After dark, Cochrane did all the steering; while down in the engine-room were Looney as mechanic, and Old

Man and Johnny as starters. Meantime, Perce sat on
deck with his feet through the hatchway against the
clutch-lever below him. By jamming this hard down,
and tapping the clutch with a hammer, it was possible
to persuade the cones to separate when required. For over
four hours we spent our time starting and stopping. Our
two best runs lasted for thirty and thirty-five minutes.
Usually a run lasted for five or less. We took it in turns to
tap the feed-pipe with a piece of wood, in the hope of
keeping it from clogging; but it was of little use. Each time
the engines stopped, Looney took down the separator and
feed-pipe and blew through them, getting a mouthful of
paraffin for his pains. When all was ready again, the two
starters, though almost dead-beat, managed somehow to
turn the crank.

By 10 p.m. we were becoming desperate. It was only
Cochrane's cheering news that we were within two
hours' run of the coast that kept the engine-room staff
going. A run of five minutes meant a mile nearer home,
so we carried on.

An hour later, Cochrane told us all to sit on the star-
board side, for it was on this side that the feed-pipe left
the tank. This was sheer genius on his part. From that
very moment the wilful engine behaved herself, and ran
obediently till we meant her to stop.

Cochrane had altered the course to make for the western
end of the high range of mountains visible about due south
of us. When about two miles from the shore we turned
eastwards, and moved parallel to the coast, on the look-
out for a good anchorage, if possible near a village.
Finally, about a hundred yards from the shore, we dropped anchor in a wide bay.

And so we had reached Cyprus, but we were all in too
dazed a condition to realise for the moment what it
meant; in fact, it took many days to do so. On arrival in

the bay, Cochrane, with his keen sense of smell, had declared that there were cows not far off, and at about 3 o'clock we heard a cock crow. We said we would eat our hats, or words to that effect, if we did not have that bird for breakfast. There was not a single light on shore, and we had no idea whereabouts in Cyprus we had dropped anchor. As the stars disappeared in the coming light of dawn, we saw the coast more clearly. Then by degrees what we thought were ruins on the coast, rocks a couple of hundred yards east of us took form; later these proved to be the still occupied Greek monastery of Acropedi. Then a house or two near by stood distinct; then trees; and finally our eyes beheld not a mile away a large village, boasting churches, mosques, and fine buildings set in trees, and beyond a mountain-range rising sheer from the very houses.

With the first light came a man to the beach opposite us. We shouted to him in English, French, and Turkish, but he appeared not to understand. Soon he was joined by two or three others. Then they started arriving in tens and twenties, men, women, and children. Mounted gendarmes galloped down. We shouted ourselves hoarse, but to no purpose. We tried several times to start up the motor, but we could not turn the handle. Finally Cochrane jumped overboard in a shirt borrowed for the occasion, as it was longer and less torn than his own. He must have felt still rather undressed for the ordeal, as when he reached the water he shouted for his hat, which was thrown to him. Clothed thus he swam towards the shore. In two feet of water his courage gave way, and his modesty made him sit down. So situated he harangued the crowd.

Finally there appeared a gendarme who understood English. He said there was an English police officer in the village, which was named Lapethos; so borrowing a pencil and a piece of paper, Cochrane wrote a note to the Englishman reporting our arrival. He explained to the gendarme that we wanted to bring the boat ashore, but that we could not start the engine. When this was understood several men at once stripped and swam out to the rest of us. Cochrane came back smoking a cigarette, which he passed round when he got on board. The Cypriots too brought cigarettes perched behind their ear like a clerk's pencil, and these we smoked with great appreciation. The scheme was for us to weigh the anchor, give the men towing-ropes, and they would then pull the boat inshore. The men, though small, were well built. As they had started swimming almost before they could walk, it was no hardship for them to tow our heavy vessel. Laughing and shouting, they pulled us along until they thought a rest would be pleasant, then they came on board again. They shouted now and then in sheer lightness of heart; they were very cheery fellows. We were not towed straight inshore, but to a small natural jetty a hundred and fifty yards west of us along the beach.

Here we stepped on British soil, eight thin and weary ragamuffins. We know our hearts gave thanks to God, though our minds could not grasp that we were really free.

The eight escapers travelled home in three separate groups, were received by the King, and then met for a celebration dinner. The date of their reunion was 11th November, 1918: Armistice Night.

12

The Escape of the Tchernavin family, from Soviet Russia to Finland, summer, 1931

In 1930 Madame Tchernavin's husband, a professor at St Petersburg University, was arrested, and in February of the following year she was herself taken away to prison, but was released five months later. That summer her husband was transferred from a penal camp to do research in marine zoology on the shores of the White Sea, under police supervision. She was allowed to visit him there with her young son. Two days before her permit expired they set out to walk a hundred miles through swamps and forests, to the Finnish border. They lost their compass and map soon after setting out, and had to press on with nothing but hope and instinct to guide them.

The boy dropped asleep the moment he swallowed his last spoonful; his face looked rosy and, as it were, rounder, after food. We sat by the fire, talking.

It was our first real conversation since we escaped.

Only that evening, by the fire, we ventured at last to speak of what lay before us. A warm and happy sense of intimacy descended upon us; long forgotten thoughts and feelings rose in our minds and our far-off youth seemed to have returned to us once more. Timidly, and as it were, shyly, we began to think of the future.

The next day our journey grew more difficult. The beautiful pine forest came to an end, and we had once

146

more to go up and down ravines and valleys. The sun came out occasionally, but it was difficult to find the way because the whole place was cut up by mountain ridges, big and small, going in different directions. It was becoming more and more doubtful whether we should ever find the Finnish River which was to guide us.

'The only thing we can do is to go towards the west,' I insisted.

'But we can't go climbing all these mountain chains,' my husband said. 'We must find a good-sized valley and take our bearing from there.'

He and the boy climbed up a hill and came down, very pleased.

'Some ten miles away there's a river which seems to run south, and there's a lot of leafy trees near it. It's a fine valley. If we are in Finland already, we need not be afraid of going south.'

We reached the river after making several *détours* because of marshes, a wide side-stream, and so on. We found that it flowed north and if we followed it we would come right back into Russia.

It was a great blow to us. The river bank was one continuous marsh overgrown with wiry Arctic birch. The bank opposite tempted us by its white moss and pretty fir trees. We decided to wade across to it. We were exhausted, chilled to the bone, got a lot of our things wet, and found ourselves in a worse marsh than ever. We managed to light a bonfire under an uprooted fir tree and kept it up through half the night to dry a place where we could sleep.

The morning was damp and foggy.

'We must stay here till the sun comes out,' my husband said.

'We must go on, for we shall never see the sun in this swamp,' I objected.

After much hesitation we decided to go on. We came

147

upon the same river which took another turn, waded across it and climbed uphill.

'I am not going to move from here till the sun comes out,' said my husband.

We lit a bonfire and sadly lay down beside it. It came on to rain several times during the night. Our Soviet water-proofs let water through quite freely. The fire hissed, fighting the rain. It was a bad look-out.

I was awakened by a sharp exclamation of my husband's. He was standing and pointing with a bitter laugh to the flat red disc of the sun rising from behind the very hill which we thought was in the west.

So the whole journey of the previous day had been wasted. We had to wade through the chilly river once more and climb to the place which we had left two evenings before.

A higher ridge rising high above the line of the forest, and a perfect chaos of valleys and smaller ridges lay before us.

Our position was very serious. It had taken us eight days, instead of three or four, to reach the frontier; three-quarters of our provisions, intended for ten days, were gone, and we were beginning to feel exhausted. Though we were safe now from pursuit and from frontier guards, we might easily perish in Finland if we did not find a way out of these wilds and come across human habitation.

Now we dragged ourselves along rather than walked. Our feet were in an awful condition – bruised, swollen, with festering wounds. Before starting a day's march we had to spend no end of time bandaging them; I had to tear up my chemise to make bandages, and every evening we discovered fresh sores.

We were suffering from hunger, too. We reduced our daily portion to two or three tablespoonfuls of rice and two ounces of bacon which we added to the mushroom soup in the morning and evening. The rusks were finished.

We had two lumps of sugar a day, one in the morning and one in the evening, and the boy had a third in the middle of the day.

A fresh misfortune was the cold. A north wind was blowing continually, and we were simply frozen in the night if we could not find enough dry wood to feed the fire all the time.

On one of those cold nights my husband had another attack of pains, and in the morning he found he could not use his left arm. He felt breathless, and when the pains came on again was not able to walk. We thought it was probably his heart. Over-strained by the life in the penal camp, by our march (we were already twelve days on the way) and the heavy weight he carried, it might give way any day. And what would become of us then?

Our only salvation would be to meet some one. We talked of nothing but where and how we could find any people.

Sixteen days after they set out, they came to an empty forest hut. By this time they were hungry and exhausted. The man decided he must go on alone and find help. 'I will find people in a couple of days.' He kissed his wife's hands; she gave him her wedding ring, the child's photograph, two sugarlumps, a teaspoonful of salt, and two ounces of bacon – 'There was nothing more to give.' He set off. The woman and the child were to wait six days. For most of the first day the boy slept.

There were lots of logs and branches lying about. I brought in heaps and heaps of them, badly scratching my hands, but I knew that all this burned very quickly: the chief thing was to find two tree trunks that would keep the fire going all night. At first I thought I could not move them at all; then I dragged them for two paces and fell down, but eventually they were in the hut, though my arms and legs were trembling with the effort. Our supper was ready, but the boy could not swallow more than two or three spoonfuls.

'I can't eat; it makes me rather sick.'

'Here's a little salt for you; put it on your palm and when you begin to feel bad, have a lick.'

'Right. Yes, it tastes quite good.'

We got through our supper in this way and the boy went to sleep. Now I understood what keeping up a fire through the night means! At first the branches caught quickly, throwing off a tremendous heat, and I dropped asleep, overcome by the warmth; then the fire died down, the cold of the night crept nearer and nearer, but I had not the strength to wake up. At last, when I opened my eyes, it was dark, bright stars were shining in the clear sky, the burnt branches showed black, and the two tree trunks underneath crackled, sending up pungent white smoke. I had to make haste and put some more on; the branches were all tangled into a heap, and if I put on too many I could not blow up the fire. I felt very sorry for myself, but could not give up the job because the boy was shivering in his sleep. I broke up some twigs, shovelled the hot embers under them, put branches at the top and blew, and blew, and blew. The white ashes flew about in flakes, clouds of white smoke rose up, two or three tongues of pale orange flame showed through the smoke and the whole heap blazed up suddenly.

That sort of thing went on all night, almost every half-hour.

How I longed for morning, sunshine, and steady warmth! Meanwhile, in the cold light of the moon everything sparkled with silvery hoar-frost.

Our second day began late – the child did not wake till nine, having gone to sleep at seven the evening before. I had burnt up all my supplies of firewood, my hands were black and grey, but, anyway, the boy had been warm while he slept.

'I wonder where Daddy is now?' he said with a sigh as soon as he woke up. 'I could have walked all right to-day.'

But when I made him wash himself and then put him out in the sun, he dropped asleep again.

The second, the third, and the fourth days were exactly like the first.

The next day would be the sixth since my husband left. If he did not return, we should have to set off after midday. What should I say to the boy? How could we go, knowing that his father had perished?

The boy was the first to wake up that morning.

'Will Daddy come back to-day, Mother?'

'I don't know, dear; perhaps to-morrow.'

'You know, we have one lump of sugar left? Don't let us eat it till Daddy comes back.'

'Very well.'

'Only, please, Mother, don't go away.'

'But I must pick some berries to make our tea.'

'Then I'll stand by the hut and sing, and you answer me.'

'All right.'

I wandered about and he stood by the hut and sang. His clear voice echoed down the river, and sometimes I called back to him.

He called to me once:

'Mother, listen, there are voices!'

'No, darling, it's your fancy.'

During those days we had heard voices, and singing, and music, but it was all an hallucination.

'Please, don't go away, Mother,' he said anxiously.

'I'll come to you in a minute. I'll only pick the bilberries under that pine tree.'

I went a little way, to hear the better. Voices. Loud

men's voices. It was not he. If it had been he, he would have let us know by calling in his own special way.

'Mother!' the child cried with all his might.

I was already running to the hut.

Two men in military uniform were coming out of the forest at a quick pace. But where was *he*? There! He was staggering, his face looked dreadful, black and swollen, and there was some dry blood near the nose.

'Darling, darling!' We held his hands again, the boy was kissing and stroking him.

He sank helplessly on the logs without looking at us.

'Dearest, what has happened?'

'I had a fall and hurt myself. Give me some water.'

'Here, Daddy, have a drink. Mother will make tea directly; we saved up one teaspoonful and a lump of sugar.'

'It took me two days to get there, though I had nothing to eat and my boots had fallen to pieces. They thought they would walk quicker than I did, but I could scarcely drag them here! They took three days on the way.'

Naturally, they could not walk like a man who is trying to save all that he holds dear in life.

There was a rattle in his throat, he coughed, and fresh blood showed on his handkerchief that was already stained with red.

'I hurt myself when I fell,' he said guiltily.

'Was the journey difficult?'

'Very. A lot of stones.'

The boy hugged and kissed his father and was almost in tears. He could not understand what the matter was – why was Daddy so strange, as though he weren't glad.

Meanwhile the Finns cooked some oatmeal porridge. They shared it with us in a brotherly way and also gave each of us a piece of black bread. It is curious that only the taste of real food makes one understand how hungry one is. We felt that we could have sat there eating for a long, long time. But the porridge was soon gone.

'How are your feet? Can you walk?' my husband asked. 'Their provisions are coming to an end; we'll have to hurry.'

'Yes, we can walk all right. Our feet are much better.'

When we were among the thick elm and willow bushes some five hundred yards away from the hut, my husband asked me:

'Did one of you sing?'

'Yes. The boy sang, and I answered him.'

'Just at this spot I heard your voices, but I thought it was my fancy. I had imagined so many times that I heard you talking and singing. But this time it was wonderfully clear. These men had been making difficulties since yesterday; they were frightened and decided that I was a Bolshevik, leading them into a trap. This morning they gave me two hours: if we did not reach the hut within that time they would turn back and make me go with them or kill me. Two hours had passed and they began to bar my way. And suddenly I heard a voice: it was the boy singing. Then the wind carried it away. I lost my head completely and started to run towards the sound. I fell, scrambled on to my feet, and ran again. They would certainly have shot me, but then they too heard the voice. I was in such an agony of despair that I am not myself yet. . . . Had they turned back you would have both perished. You could never have found your way alone, and to-day is the sixth day, so you would have concluded that I was dead. And indeed I would have been dead, for I certainly would not have turned back alive. I've never lived through anything more terrible. . . . Now they will lead us to safety; but I can't get over it yet.'

'You will, in time,' said I. 'The only thing that matters is that you have saved us.'

13

The Escape of Wing-Commander Basil Embry, R.A.F., from Occupied France, 27th May to 23rd July, 1940

This account was written in 1945 by A. J. Evans, himself a celebrated escaper of World War I.

On 27th May, 1940, W./C. Embry baled out of his Blenheim from about 4000 feet and descended into an orchard near St Omer. He was unhurt except for a piece of shell which had lodged in the fleshy part of his leg. At first this wound gave him little trouble, and I do not think he ever asked the Germans for medical attention. Many Germans were in and around the orchard, so there was no chance of evasion, and he was soon in their hands. Once they learned his rank he was treated with becoming dignity, and in due course was transported in General Guderian's own staff car to the German H.Q. Here he was put in the charge of a young staff officer who spoke excellent English and was responsible for Embry's safe retention. It was also this officer's job to extract as much military information from his guest as could be obtained by tactful means.

That evening they had dinner together, and over a bottle of wine swapped lies till midnight. Embry at any rate drew freely on an extensive imagination and doubtless the German did the same. The rather tough examination of prisoners which was usual in the latter part of the war was not then part of the German system. Embry had a particularly nimble brain, so it is more than probable that he deceived the Germans on many points and gave nothing away.

Next day, after an uncomfortable night in a stable, Embry was removed from headquarters in a staff car – decanted from this into a lorry and finally arrived at a dirty prisoner-of-war cage walking on his flat feet in the pouring rain. Conditions in all German concentration camps in those days were much the same, for it is probable that the Germans never anticipated capturing so many prisoners, particularly French prisoners – who were invariably treated far better than the British.

In this camp Embry met F./Lt. Treacy, who had been shot down near Calais a few days before. These two decided to take the first opportunity of escaping together. A couple of days later they found themselves tramping eastwards along the roads of France as members of a long column of prisoners of war. The Irish undoubtedly have a natural gift for this type of adventure, and both Embry and Treacy were Irish. This column of prisoners was particularly well guarded; very little straggling was permitted, and it was noticeable that as the column passed through woods or villages there was always a marked increase in the activity and vigilance of the guards.

In the German army there is a well-recognised army manual method of guarding columns of prisoners. It was not always used, owing to lack of necessary transport, but in this case it was in full operation. At the head of the column there was a lorry on which was mounted a machine gun and crew, followed at about a hundred and fifty yards interval by other lorries, also with machine guns, and so on, down the column – the tail being brought along and stragglers rounded up by a few troops with rifles and tommy guns. A sidecar combination on which a machine gun was mounted was attached to the column. This man's operational method was to come past the prisoners from behind and then to take up a convenient position from where he could watch the prisoners pass. He would then repeat the manoeuvre. The impression that this made upon a prisoner was of a succession of motor-cyclists passing the column at frequent intervals, though in reality it was always the same man. It must be owned that the above is a remarkably efficient method of guarding prisoners with a minimum of effort.

Embry and Treacy soon came to the conclusion that the best time to make an attempt to escape was when the column was marching on a long, straight road, for that was the only time when the attention of the guards relaxed. The strain of waiting for hours for a chance to escape is, as I know myself, very great. There seems always to be half a chance – never a whole one. The prospective escaper is continually screwing himself up to the necessary pitch and then again relaxing with a simultaneous feeling of relief and disappointment each time he decides that an opportunity is unacceptable.

Treacy and Embry were being marched along one of the poplar-lined roads of France, keyed up to take the first chance that offered, when Embry saw at the side of the road a signpost on which was written his own name – marvellous to relate, there was a village called Embry. He instantly decided that this was his cue, and without hesitation dived out of the column and lay still in the ditch at the side of the road. Cover was of the poorest and he was exposed to view, but no one had seen him go. Dead men at the side of the road are not an uncommon sight, so the column moved on and left him lying there unnoticed.

Treacy told me that Embry dived from the column

like a shot out of a gun and left him 'all standing'. It was perhaps just as well that both of them did not attempt to escape at the same moment, for if they had done so they could have hardly avoided being seen.

A few hundred yards farther on Treacy also escaped. He and Embry took totally different paths, and in fact never saw each other again till they met some months later as free men once more in the Royal Air Force in England. [*Treacy was later killed.*]

Meanwhile, Embry lay in an uncomfortable and exposed position by the main road on which there was a considerable amount of German traffic. The only cover he could see was a wood some three hundred yards away across a field. He determined to make an attempt to reach the wood. In the field was an old woman milking a cow and it now appeared that she alone had seen his escape from the column, for she looked towards him as he started to crawl, and then signalled to him with her hand when he should move forward and when he should lie still. Thus, by slow degrees and largely owing to the courageous help of this old woman, he edged himself across the field till at last he reached the cover of the wood.

The next ten days were pretty grim. That part of the country where he found himself was infested with Germans; they seemed to be in every farm-house and almost in every wood, and the peasants and small farmers were usually too frightened to give help. He found great difficulty in getting food and reasonable civilian clothes, without which it was impossible to move about in the daytime. At last he acquired a pair of blue trousers from a farmer and took an old coat off a scarecrow and, thus equipped, made better progress. During these ten days Embry seldom entered a house. The weather was often wet, and to add to his troubles he was in great pain from the wound in his leg. As there was no chance of any proper medical assistance, he was compelled to operate on his leg with a penknife – a most unpleasant and painful experience which exhausted him so much that he lay up for two days in a wet wood, trying to recover his strength and almost unable to move. There is no doubt that Embry must have been exceptionally tough to have survived those ten days. Starving, wet through continually, with a painful wound, alone in a country crawling with Germans, his position was pretty desperate.

Many men – even good escapers – would, I think, have surrendered under such conditions; for there comes a time when the body, its resistance reduced by starvation and exposure, affects the mind and reduces the strength of the will. Gradually, imperceptibly, the fear of death and particularly a lonely death, overcomes the desire for freedom. This does not necessarily lead to surrender but the arguments in favour of it become gradually stronger as the body grows weaker. That at any rate was my own experience, but I have no idea whether Embry ever contemplated giving himself up – it may be he never even wavered in his determination.

Whatever were his thoughts during those desperate days, we find him about a fortnight after his escape from the column, walking south along the roads of France clad in blue trousers and scarecrow coat, and apparently completely recovered.

Embry's normal appearance is not such as would mark him as particularly British. On the contrary, in non-British clothes he would pass easily as a native in almost any part of the continent of Europe.

He is about 5 feet 8 inches in height, with a well-knit frame and square, powerful shoulders. He is very dark, with thick black hair and a complexion to match. A notable feature are his eyes which are blue and singularly bright and he has the habit of fixing anyone to whom he speaks with a penetrating and, until you are used to it – an almost embarrassing gaze. In the nonde-script clothing such as he wore on his walk through France, he would pass naturally as a bombed-out refugee (of which numbers were wandering about), without arousing the least suspicion, and this was the rôle he adopted.

From time to time he was stopped by German controls and asked for his papers, but for the most part these incidents presented no serious difficulties to an unusually intelligent man whose appearance was in his favour. When questioned he would throw up his arms and in passable French, give a harrowing if incoherent description of the destruction of his village by German bombs. 'No, he had no papers – they had all been blown up together with his wife and family . . . and now he was hunting for his old mother who had last been heard of in this district.'

Some such story as this – varied to taste – passed muster without much difficulty. There were so many refugees with true stories somewhat resembling the above, that it was impossible in the still hopelessly disorganised state of France, for the normal German, untrained in counter-espionage, to distinguish the false from the true.

One day he was passing through a village in his usual inconspicuous way when he heard behind him the ringing footsteps of three men marching in step. He stood aside to let them pass. To his dismay, he realised instantly that the men were British tommies, dressed, it is true, in civilian clothes, but marching straight to captivity. He took the great risk of stopping them and giving them some sane advice, but unfortunately they had already drawn suspicion upon themselves. A few minutes later, Embry and the three soldiers were arrested and separated from each other. Embry was brought before a German officer to whom he explained as usual, that he was a Belgian refugee.

To his horror the German, who turned out to be an interpreter, addressed him in fluent and seemingly perfect French without, as yet, showing any signs of disbelief. Embry felt that this could not continue, and in order to cover his own poor French, quickly explained that his native tongue was Flemish. The interpreter instantly addressed him in Flemish, of which language Embry knew not one single word.

The situation was desperate, because once caught telling lies, a closer and probably fatal examination would surely follow.

'Hush,' said Embry, taking the interpreter aside, 'I must confess I have not been telling the truth. I am a Gael.'

'A Gael? What's that? I've never heard of one,' answered the astonished interpreter. 'Where do they come from?'

'From Southern Ireland,' said Embry, inventing rapidly.

'Well, that's interesting. But what are you doing here?'

'Hush, I'm running away from the London Police. I have been in England, blowing up pillar boxes and the police are on my track.'

'Grand fellow,' said the interpreter patting him on the back enthusiastically. 'Good luck to your great work. You talk Gaelic, of course?' he added, as a slight suspicion entered his mind.

'Naturally,' said Embry, 'it's my native tongue.'

'Well, say something in Gaelic then,' the interpreter told him.

Without hesitation Embry proceeded to let off the few sentences in Urdu which he knew by heart as the result of a sojourn in the East.

'Good,' said the interpreter, 'that's Gaelic. I speak a little myself.'

To his great surprise, Embry found himself once more

free to continue his journey towards Paris. . . .

During his walk through France, some of the time in company with the advancing German troops, Embry made fullest use of his eyes and his memory. He went out of his way to lie up beside aerodromes and noted their methods of organisation for defence and dispersal. He saw their columns bombed on the roads and saw how our plan of attack could be improved, so that on his return, he was able to put in a report giving detailed information of the German habits and recommendations for improvements in our methods of attack.

One could only wish that all escapers had used their opportunities as well as he did.

The story of Embry's adventures and contacts as he walked through France does not differ greatly from that of many other evaders. He seems to have passed through a country infested with Germans with little difficulty, and it was an ill chance that landed him once more in the hands of the enemy. He had just swum the Somme and was crossing a field when, in the dark, he ran straight into a number of German soldiers. He was instantly collared and beaten up, and finally, after a most unpleasant and painful experience, was taken before a German officer to whom he told his usual – and now familiar – tale. The German made the following answer.

'I don't believe a word of what you say. I think you are a British officer trying to escape. You are in civilian clothes so that, if you are what I think you are, you will be shot as a spy tomorrow.'

After these discouraging remarks, Embry was led away to a large farm-house which proved to be a German H.Q. This farm was of the normal type to be found everywhere in northern France. The building formed three sides of a square and the fourth side consisted of a wall in which was the main gate. In the middle of the courtyard was an enormous manure heap on which ducks, chickens and pigs roamed at will. About midday, Embry was deposited in a small room, normally used for storage purposes. A sentry was placed over the door and a second sentry stood in the courtyard outside the only exit.

After carefully considering his position, Embry came to the conclusion that his chances of being shot the following morning were distinctly promising; for the possibility of passing successfully through an interrogation made by a competent man who spoke French well, was almost nil. His story would be exposed as a lie, and with the German suspicions aroused, he could think of no other story likely to hold water. He could talk no other language but English sufficiently well to pass as a native. He had been caught in the German lines dressed in civilian clothes, so he could see no good reason why he should not be shot as a spy. (In actual fact, the Geneva Convention lays down that the question of whether a man is a spy or not is a question of fact which must be proved against a prisoner before he can be legitimately shot.) Many airmen have baled out over German occupied territory in this war, have changed into civilian clothes and have subsequently been caught by the Germans; but none, as far as I know, have been shot as a spy merely for being in civilian clothes. However, the Germans were often in doubt on this matter, and from time to time posted up notices threatening to shoot all combatants found out of uniform, but never carried out this threat. In acting thus, I have always thought that the Germans behaved with a leniency and moderation which is frankly surprising, considering the depths to which they descended in shooting and torturing the unfortunate natives who gave assistance to our evaders. All this Embry could not have known at the time, but I am inclined to agree with his view that in his particular circumstances he was unlikely to receive the benefit of any doubt.

Having come to the conclusion that his position was really desperate, Embry was the last man to take it lying down.

He asked his sentry for a glass of water and when he returned with it, hit him as hard as he could on the point of the jaw. He took the rifle and having made sure that this sentry was 'out' in a satisfactory manner, he advanced cautiously down the passage. Just outside the exit into the court-yard was a second sentry with his back towards him. As Embry came out, the man turned and at that moment Embry hit him with his full force on the side of the head with the butt of the rifle. His head caved in, and Embry rushed along the side of the building towards the gate, clutching the rifle. There was no one about in the court-yard. Just as he came to a passage between the two buildings, a German soldier came round the corner carrying two buckets of water, and stood for a second, a look of intense astonishment on his face. Embry hit him, too, in the same manner and with the same result, and then, there being nothing else for it, dived into the manure heap and dug a passage for himself through the straw and well into the muck. It was not long before the hue and cry started, but no one thought of the manure heap – perhaps no one thought it possible that a man could live in it.

Many hours later, during the night, he crawled out of the manure and got out of the court-yard without being observed – heaven knows how he did it. Once more he was on the roads of France, making his way toward Paris in close company with the German army, also marching in the same direction. One cannot help imagining that he smelt strongly of manure.

A few days later he found an old bicycle shop full of odds and ends and bits of bicycles. After two days hard work, he constructed a bicycle out of odd pieces and on it made much more rapid progress until the bicycle was commandeered from him by a German soldier. At this time his wounded leg began to swell up and give him great pain. Nevertheless he finished the journey to Paris on foot. Paris was full of German troops, but Embry passed inconspicuously, a dirty, ragged, limping figure, through the streets. For some reason he had great difficulty in finding the American Embassy. When at last he succeeded in finding it, he put on a slight American accent and attempted to pass himself off as a citizen of the USA who had been bombed-out and overwhelmed by the advancing German armies. He was interviewed by a sharp young American girl who mistrusted either his accent or his story and accused him without hesitation of being a British officer in disguise. When he confessed the truth, he was told that it was not in the power of the Embassy to give him much help. He was lent a few hundred francs with the advice to apply to the Salvation Army HQ. His subsequent adventures in Paris are complicated and obscure. For several days he was locked up in a barred cage under stinking conditions, with all the riff-raff of the criminal underworld. For many days he walked the streets disclosing his identity to prosperous-looking Frenchmen and borrowing money from them. He also entered shops and asked them to lend him money. Money was a necessity, either for purposes of bribery or to enable him to obtain a bicycle.

At last, after a terrible time in Paris he, by some means, got hold of a bicycle and in one day rode to the neighbourhood of Tours – a distance of 145 miles. As an athletic feat this was a truly remarkable performance, because his leg, now swollen to double its normal size, was giving him great pain. At Limoges he was given help by some French officers, but by now his leg was so bad he could hardly walk. He went into hospital for a few days, but dared not stay, because the Germans might arrive in the town at any time, so with French help he went on, in spite of his condition, to Toulouse and thence to Marseilles.

With a special pass obtained from French friends he journeyed from Marseilles to a small port on the coast, near Perpignan, where he and two other escapers attempted to steal a boat with the object of reaching Barcelona. They were arrested by the French police and spent the night with the Foreign Legion. By this time his physical condition was really desperate and he began to wonder whether, even if he succeeded in escaping, he would not lose his leg, or possibly his life. When he had reached the very limit of his endurance and was no longer capable of physical exertion, help arrived.

This was towards the end of June. A brave French girl, Anne-Louise, tended his leg which responded to treatment and began to heal. From Marseilles and Perpignan he eventually reached the town of Le Perthous on the Spanish frontier. After many delays, a British agent who was a Gibraltarian succeeded in smuggling him across the frontier in the boot of his car. He arrived in Madrid on 24th July, 1940.

Embry ended his Air Force career as Air Chief Marshal Sir Basil Embry, K.C.B., K.B.E., D.S.O. and three bars, D.F.C., A.F.C. (holding in addition four foreign decorations), Air Officer Commanding-in-Chief of Fighter Command.

14

The Escape of Lieutenant Pierre Mairesse Lebrun, of the French cavalry, from Colditz Castle in Germany, 1st July, 1941

The escape of Lieutenant Lebrun, Officer of the Légion d'Honneur, Croix de Guerre, M.C., is here described by one of his fellow-prisoners, Major P. R. Reid.

Lieutenant Mairesse Lebrun was a French cavalry officer, tall, handsome, and debonair, and a worthy compatriot of that famed cuirassier of Napoleon whose legendary escapades were so ably recounted by Conan Doyle in his book, *The Adventures of Brigadier Gerard.*

Lebrun had slipped the German leash from Colditz once already by what seems, in the telling, a simple ruse. In fact, it required quite expert handling. A very small Belgian officer was his confederate. On one of the 'Park' outings the Belgian officer concealed himself under the voluminous folds of a tall comrade's cloak at the outgoing 'numbering off' parade and was not counted. During the recreation period in the Park, Lebrun, with the aid of suitable diversions, climbed up among the rafters of an open-sided pavilion situated in the middle of the recreation pen. He was not missed because the Belgian provided the missing number, and the dogs did not get wind of him. Later he descended and, smartly dressed in a grey flannel suit sent by a friend from

France, he walked to a local railway station and proffered a hundred-mark note at the booking-office in exchange for a ticket. Unfortunately, the note was an old one, no longer in circulation. The station-master became suspicious and finally locked Lebrun up in a cloakroom and telephoned the camp. The Camp Commandant replied that nothing was amiss and that his prisoner complement was complete. While he was phoning, Lebrun wrenched open a window and leaped out on top of an old woman, who naturally became upset and gave tongue. A chase ensued. He was finally cornered by the station personnel and recaptured. In due course he was returned to the Castle and handed over to the protesting Commandant.

This adventure lost Mairesse his fine suit and found him doing a month's 'solitary' confinement at the same time as Peter Allan.

One fine afternoon we heard many shots fired in the playground and rushed to the windows, but could see nothing because of the foliage. Terrific excitement followed in the German quarters and we saw posses of Goons with dogs descending at the double from the Castle and disappearing among the trees. Shouts and orders and the barking of dogs continued for some time and eventually faded away in the distance.

We heard by message from Peter Allan what had happened. The 'solitaries' – at the time a mere half a dozen – were having their daily exercise in the park, during which period they could mix freely. Being only a few, they were sparsely guarded, though confined to one end of the compound, where the prisoners played football among the trees. Lebrun was in the habit of doing exercises with two other Frenchmen, which included much leapfrogging. Now Lebrun was athletic. It was high summer and he was dressed in what remained to him of his former finery – shorts, a yellow cardigan, an open-necked shirt, and gym shoes – not good escaping clothes, but that was also what he reckoned the Germans would think. While a couple of the latter were lolling rather sleepily outside the wire and looking at anything but the prisoners, Lebrun innocently leapfrogged with the other Frenchmen.

It all happened in a flash. His French colleague stood near the wire and, forming with his two hands a stirrup into which Lebrun placed his foot, he catapulted him upwards. Acrobats can heave each other tremendous distances by this method. Precision of timing of muscular effort is its secret. Lebrun and his friend managed it, and the former sailed in a headlong dive over the nine-foot wire.

This was only half the battle. Lebrun ran twenty yards along the fence to the main wall of the park. He had to reclimb the wire, using it as a ladder, in order to hoist himself on to the top of the wall which was, at this point, about thirteen feet high. Rather than present a slowly moving target during this climb, Lebrun de-liberately attracted the fire of the two nearest sentries by running backwards and forwards beside the wall. Their magazines once emptied (and having missed), the re-loading gave him the extra seconds he needed. He was on top of the wall by the time they fired again and drop-ped to the ground on the other side in a hail of bullets as the more distant sentries joined in the fusillade.

He disappeared and was never recaught. He certainly deserves the greatest credit for this escape, which was in the true French cavalry tradition and demanded the very quintessence of courage, remembering the effort was made in cold blood and with every opportunity for re-flection on the consequences of a false step. A British officer, in a similar attempt a few years later, was shot dead. The escape savours of a generation of Frenchmen of whom the majority disappeared on the battlefields of

the First World War and who, alas, never had the chance
to sire and educate a generation like themselves to follow
in their footsteps.

I met Lebrun again long afterwards, when the war was
over, and here is the end of his story.

Lebrun escaped on 1st July, 1941. Although he had
the sleuth-hounds and a posse of Goons on his tail within
ten minutes, he managed to hide in a field of wheat. (You
must walk in backwards, rearranging the stalks as you
go.) There he hid the whole afternoon with a search
plane circling continuously above him. At 10 p.m. he
set off. He had twenty German marks which were smuggled into his prison cell from the camp. He walked about
fifty miles and then stole a bicycle and cycled between
sixty and a hundred miles a day. He posed as an Italian
officer and begged or bought food at lonely farmhouses,
making sure, by a stealthy watch beforehand, that there
were only women in the house. His bicycle 'sprang a
leak', so he abandoned it and stole a second. On the
journey to the Swiss frontier he was stopped twice by
guards and ran for it each time. On the second occasion,
about twenty-five miles from the frontier, he tripped the
guard up with the aid of his bicycle and knocked him
out with his bicycle pump. He took to the woods and
crossed the frontier safely on 8th July.

Within a week he was in France. In December 1942
he crossed the Pyrenees and was taken prisoner by the
Spaniards, who locked him up in a castle. He jumped
from a window into the moat and broke his spine on
some rocks at the bottom, was removed, laid down on a
mattress, and left to die. A local French consul, however,
who had previously been endeavouring to extricate the
incarcerated Lebrun, heard of the accident and insisted
on an immediate operation. Lebrun's life was saved. He
eventually reached Algeria to carry on the war. Today,

though permanently crippled by his fall, he is a pillar in his own country.

If any German had examined Lebrun's cell at Colditz when he left for his daily exercise on 1st July, he might have nipped Lebrun's escape in the bud. Lebrun had packed up his belongings and addressed them to himself in France. Months later they arrived – forwarded by Oberst-leutnant Prawitt, the Colditz Camp Commandant!

15

The Escape of Flight Lieutenant O. L. S. Philpot, R.A.F., from Stalag Luft III at Sagan, 29th October, 1943

Flight Lieutenant Oliver Philpot was the third man in the cele-
brated 'Wooden Horse' escape which was planned by Flight
Lieutenant E. E. Williams, R.A.F., and Lieutenant R. M. C.
Codner, of the Royal Artillery; all three men were to be awarded
the M.C. for this escape. In the summer of 1943 Philpot was
appointed escape co-ordinator for Hut 62 at Sagan, and one day
Williams and Codner told him their idea for a tunnel beginning
out in the open compound, its entrance masked by a portable,
home-made vaulting horse. He put the idea forward and it was
approved. Later he accepted an invitation to be the third man in
the team of three. Williams and Codner began tunnelling on
8th July, 1943, and the three men broke out on 29th October.

It was the Compound's church choir of P.O.Ws that
saved us. They came trooping into the music-room, bliss-
fully unconscious of any special event being 'on', until
told roughly, 'Go on, chaps, sing if you're going to.'
They found some of their music mysteriously taken from
their hands by P.O.W.s to whom they had never spoken
before, and who remained stolidly by their side; the
piano struck up in preparation for the next Sunday, and
a far larger choir than originally planned, and one even
more intent on its singing, sang something about 'And

His Angels shall uphold and guide thee', and sang it lustily.

Charlie, the ferret, came and looked in the window. He peered around, and departed. Church choirs had never given him much trouble; he was not particularly interested.

'Right,' said David, putting down his music. 'Get going.'

The horse had never been taken out with three men in it before. I sat on one beam, Bill [*Williams*] on the other. A nippy little New Zealander named McKay was jammed more or less in mid-air between us. Up, creak, creak, and out. We formed a human octopus of hands, legs, and arms. Now we were nearly there and then down. It was infernally difficult to operate due to lack of space, but there was one of the anchor sand-bags, we could just feel it. Our helpers had found the right spot all right; usually Bill or Mike [*Codner*] did this.

Bill went down and took up a bottle of hot tea for Mike. Report came back that Mike was well, flourishing, in fact. The tunnel didn't smell too fuggy.

Bill and Mike sent down a few basins of sand from the face. I rested at the top, inside the horse, and let McKay do the work of bag filling. Better he got tired than I.

The daylight began to fail. David was in charge on the surface among the vaulters. 'Soon now,' he said and, shortly after, quietly, 'I think I should pack up now. Good luck.'

McKay called up the tunnel that we were closing down. He handed the last sand-bag up to me for hanging in the horse, and squeezed past me into the belly of the animal.

It was extraordinarily similar to plunging into a really cold sea. Hesitation was fatal. Trying hard to look nonchalant I said, 'Thanks, Mac,' and got down into the vertical shaft.

'Good luck, boy,' from Mac, a small figure looking rather forlorn, because he would like to have been on this too. 'You'll be all right.'

By then I had squirmed around sufficiently in my bulky clothing to work my way up the horizontal shaft. As I crawled up it the sounds of the outside world were clipped off – the chatter of the vaulting team could no longer be heard.

I paused for a moment, with my cheek on my arm and my chin in the dank sand. There it was. First one board, then the other. Both pushed firmly into place. No glimmer of light from the entrance now; it was completely dark.

Two thuds followed – and then a third. The anchor sand-bags were being put into position on top of the boards to hold them down. We were now firmly sealed into our tunnel, and there could be no going back.

I experienced a feeling of blind, seething rebellion at the whole thing – but got over it. I crawled up the tunnel; there was work to be done.

Our escape from Stalag Luft III had begun.

For the last time I squirmed past the very narrow bit of tunnel as it rose clear of the patch where the impact of the Stalag Luft III vaulters was heaviest. About half-way along I called to Bill and got a muffled answer.

Mike was at the very end, past the wire altogether. Bill lay approximately under the outer fence, where the tunnel had lately been bent to the right. I was third man and remained in the middle of the tunnel, under the danger-strip.

Bill passed down some basins of sand to me. We still had some digging time left and Mike was forging ahead. Also, the tunnel needed clearing, as Mike had spent the afternoon by pushing on and massing a great heap of sand behind him.

The basin jammed. Bill cursed. I cursed. A wooden

rake which I had brought down had got tangled in the basin rope. We freed it. My plan was to take sand from Bill by emptying the basins which he sent down; I would then smooth the sand out in front of me and to the sides, would scoop it back past my body and then draw myself forward over it. The rake was to smooth it out behind me, if possible, so as to leave it as flat as could be just in case some early morning vaulters were lucky enough to be able to use the hole again.

I abandoned the rake.

Bill and Mike together accumulated sand and I pulled back basin after basin. It was more difficult pulling it from the prone position than from the normal sitting position at the entrance of the tunnel.

While Bill and Mike filled the basin I felt over my clothing and equipment in the blackness. I wore my complete Norwegian outfit, my suit, shirt, collar and tie, shoes, and so on. Over the top of everything was my dyed Red Cross vest, and Red Cross long underpants; over my shoes a large extra pair of socks. All three of us wore this dark outer covering which we hoped would not show up in the lights.

I felt the scarf round my neck. I wanted to tear it off, it was so hot. It was adequately in place, protecting my collar. I felt through the wollen vest for the safety-pin fastening of my right-hand jacket pocket. It was secure, and there were the papers, forming quite a bundle, upon which Dean & Dawson had worked for so many months. On the other side was my tunnel-exit equipment, the dark helmet made of Red Cross material with the armour-like slits for the eyes and nose; also my gloves.

Jimmie's £28 10s. Rolex showed up clearly on my wrist. It was a comforting glow – a glow conveying stability and orderliness – rather like the encouraging luminous dials of the Beaufort instruments when over the North Sea it was utterly black outside the aircraft and I didn't dare to let the navigator use his light, even for a second, to look at his chart.

Down the basins came – I had kept count – five, ten, then fifteen, and now nineteen and twenty. My body swam with sweat, and the air began to get heavy, fetid, and really bad. I wondered whether to make an air-hole with a stick which I had, but the poker incident of weeks ago warned me against this. It just wouldn't do.

Gasping, I crawled up to Bill.

We had already consulted on the time at ten minutes to six (p.m.) about, forty-five minutes after we had been sealed down. It could not be long now. The foot-guard whose patrol lay on the path just above Mike was due on at 6.30 p.m. – our train was at 7 o'clock.

I yanked myself up the tunnel.

'Bill—air-hole,' I called. 'It's pretty bloody down here . . . sorry . . . but it's time for one . . . will you poke it up . . . under the coils of wire where it won't be seen?'

'No need,' Bill said. 'What's the time?'

'Just on six.'

'Thought it was about that. . . . We're breaking now. . . . Will you tie my kit-bag to my foot?'

'O.K.'

'You'll have to follow me and come up when the bag moves.'

'Right.'

I got his kit-bag out of its special wall cavity and my fingers tied it to his ankle. They seemed to work almost independently of my thinking self . . . a long way away almost. I was never very good at knots, either.

'Good luck, Bill.'

'Good luck, Ollie,' and by some contortionist feat Bill's right hand came groping back to meet mine in the sand and darkness.

'Sorry I've been such a ruddy nuisance on your Dienst,' I said. We had always argued strongly about the whole operation, and after all, it was originally Bill's and Mike's tunnel.

'Not at all, wouldn't have missed having you for worlds,' Bill whispered, which was pretty generous.

Almost as Bill spoke there was a very dull 'crump', and then another, and more. I suddenly felt my head clear as some clean air flowed in and my eyes and cheeks and neck felt cooler.

Mike had broken the tunnel. This little hole in the ground, which had become a horizontal cylinder, and then a longer and longer cylinder, had actually come up on the freedom side of the wire. After all those months, ever since early July – right through August, September – the leaves had turned – and now this was almost November.

The dull noises went on. Mike was carving the roof of the tunnel above him up there at the end. Chunks of sand were caving in, on and around him.

We didn't dare to speak any more.

In the dark I kept my hand on Bill's kit-bag. It moved. I crawled up after it.

I picked up my two parcels which were in cavities which Mike had carved.

I pushed my rolled-up R.A.F. greatcoat ahead of me, against Bill's kit-bag. My small attaché-case, containing amongst other things, John's precious Anthony Eden [*hat*], I dragged along more or less beside my knees. Both parcels were covered with the dyed Red Cross underclothing, and tied with darkened string.

The kit-bag was dragged very slowly over the sandy floor. I followed. We came to one of the very narrow bits where you couldn't get your hands underneath you in the collapsed press-up position. Once past it, I petulantly gave the wall a kick – for old times' sake as it were – it did not fall in. It was a luxury to be careless.

There were pauses. During them my whole attitude

to the tunnel suddenly changed. For months I had loathed it. It was my worst enemy – like the sea to people who hate all bodies of water. Now, as my imagination leapt ahead to the operation of getting out of it, I could only think of boundary lights, search-lights, goons in boxes, harsh excited German shouts, and, above all, that cracking, splitting noise of shots disturbing a peaceful country night. I now almost wanted to pat the tunnel – as an old dog for which I had an affection. This earthwork was now no longer enemy but friend. It gave me cover. I had air now – and it was safe, and homely; I wanted to lie prone in it for ever.

The kit-bag moved on. I had to follow. Suddenly I lost it, it moved ahead so fast. Then . . . it wasn't there at all.

I squirmed on. I came to heaps of loose sand, to the end of the tunnel. There was no sign whatsoever of Bill and Mike. I turned on my side and looked up. There was a hole and through it the night sky and, quite distinctly, the leaves of a scraggy tree near by.

There was plenty of light. I could see what I was doing. Above all, there was the silence. I could hear no noise – no shouting of guards, no firing. Bill and Mike had made it. It was now my turn.

Mike had done his stuff well. It was a good big hole, and the little den was big enough to crouch in.

I poked my head up out of the end of the Trojan Horse tunnel.

Theoretically I should be appearing in a pool of shadow, somewhere between the beams of the permanently fixed arc-lights set upon poles at intervals in the wire. In fact, I felt like an ant on a brilliantly-lit billiards table.

I glanced quickly at the nearest goon-box which was possibly eighty feet away to my left. The goon was leaning on his veranda rail, looking into the camp at all the huts behind me. I could not only see him, but could, from his attitude, sense that he was feeling more or less alert, but moody.

I pulled my head down quickly. I must be very conspicuous. As I withdrew into the hole again I caught a glimpse of the dark woods beyond. The open roadway in between looked the width of Kingsway; the sanctuary of the trees seemed a million miles away. Yet – Bill and Mike must be there, and safe!

As I crouched a swinging searchlight from one of the southern goon-boxes – was it the one bearing the name-plate 'Dietrich' – or 'Emil'? – reached out across the camp and momentarily bathed the exit of our tunnel with a brilliant glare. The angle was such that it shone direct on to one side of Mike's exit-hole, an inch or so below the surface, and lit up the sand and the tiny roots as I watched from a foot or two away within my den.

There seemed nothing to plan. This was where you wanted luck. Waiting was useless.

I pulled out my greatcoat bundle, lifted it up and through the hole, and placed it openly on top of the ground outside. I did the same with the other bundle. Without any further reconnaissance I scrambled out of the hole, bent down to pick up the two parcels, and streaked across the road.

We had always said that the thing to do was to crouch and slip over it slowly. Such plans were flung to the winds. A running target was more difficult than an ambling one.

The wood we had always regarded as thick. In practice, when I rushed into it, panting like a grampus, it had transformed itself into a sort of parkland. The few trees which were real cover were widely spaced apart; between them was low scrub through which I crashed. Go as carefully as I could I still made a noise.

Some yards inside the wood I forced myself to pull up.

There must be no further noise.

I looked back at the camp, and for the first time saw, as a free man, a prison camp from outside. The scene had something of the lighting effect of a fair at night, except that the wire stood out in sharp relief, and I could see the goons in the boxes wearing their Luftwaffe caps. I could discern the huts, and heard the clink of a water-jug, the sudden sound of P.O.W. voices in argument, and a door being banged. All familiar enough sounds.

Already I was beginning to think about the men 'in there', with me being separate and free. Although I was dripping with sweat, and tired, and was indeed merely a pin-point in an East German wood and had to get out of a closely controlled enemy country to England, hundreds of miles away, I felt suddenly a rush of buoyant confidence. I could float on air. Looking at Stalag Luft III from the outside made all the difference.

The break from the camp had succeeded.

Disguised as Jon Jorgensen, a Norwegian business man, Philpot travelled by train from Sagan to Küstrin via Frankfurt; thence to Danzig where he arrived at 5.00 p.m. on Saturday 30th October, less than 24 hours later. On the following day he climbed aboard a neutral ship, and four days later he was in Sweden. It had taken him less than a week. On 13th November, Codner and Williams, who had travelled together, also arrived at the British Legation in Stockholm. On Boxing Day Philpot was flown home, first sending to a Sagan friend a watch on which was inscribed a grinning horse with three tails, all carried high.

16

The Escape of Lieutenant Commander C. D. Smith, U.S.N.R., from Ward Road Jail, Shanghai, 6th October, 1944

Commander Smith's story was told in Officially Dead *by Quentin Reynolds. For thirteen years a shipmaster on the Yangtse River and a Shanghai pilot, Smith was re-inducted into the US Navy in March, 1941, and on 8th December was captured by the Japanese when they occupied Shanghai. With Commander John B. Woolley, D.S.C., R.N., and Commander W. S. Cunningham, U.S.N., he escaped from Woosung P.O.W. Camp on 10th March, 1942. They were re-captured within hours, tried 'for deserting from the Japanese Army', and sentenced to ten years' imprisonment. On 8th June, 1942, they were taken to Ward Road Jail, from which, at that time, no one had escaped successfully.*

Gradually we got to know some of our fellow prisoners. After four months, a delegation of marines, members of the Pekin legation guard who had been confined with us at Woosung, joined us. They had escaped, but, after seventeen days of freedom, were recaptured and sent to Bridge House for the inevitable 'questioning'. They had been starved and beaten, but they were marines and they knew how to take it. I remember the first time Woolley and I saw them. It was our exercise hour and we were walking in the yard. They came out and blinked in the bright sunlight. I looked them over appraisingly. So did Woolley. We didn't say a word but just looked at each other, and then Woolley smiled. 'You're thinking of the same thing I am, Smitty,' he said.

'That's right,' I nodded. 'That husky young marine might do nicely.'

'Well, that's what I was thinking,' he grinned.

Escape! Escape! That's all Woolley and I ever thought of. We knew it would take a miracle to accomplish it, but we were willing to believe in miracles. We had decided that a team of three would be our best bet. We needed a strong, courageous young man as our third member. This marine we were inspecting looked as though he might fill the bill.

One day we fell into conversation with the marine and pumped him cautiously. His full name was Jerold B. Storey, and he was from Bloomington, Illinois. He had gone right from high school into the Army Signal Corps and had served a three-year hitch. He had tried civilian life but evidently was one of those rare individuals who likes professional soldiering. He had joined the marines in 1940. Everything we learned about him impressed us. He was a real soldier and a husky, well-built lad.

Of course, Woolley and I still had absolutely no idea as to how we'd ever get out, but we knew we'd find a way some day. Corporal Storey began to shape up as the third member of our escape party. We decided to broach the subject to him.

'Count me in, Commander,' he said joyfully.

'You know it's beheading if we're caught, as we may well be,' I reminded him.

Storey shrugged his shoulders. 'That's all right with me, Commander,' he said.

This was our man, we decided, and nothing that ever happened afterwards changed our minds. Storey was a good marine; when you've said that there isn't much else you can say. But escape was a long way off. We formulated a dozen plans and discarded them. It would be impossible without help from outside. But if we could make friends with some criminal due to be released soon we might accomplish something. One thing we needed was to have a man working outside in the yard. I went to Mori and told him that Storey was an expert gardener and suggested that he give him a job in the vegetable garden. That was inside the big wall, of course, but it was outside the prison proper. To my surprise, Storey was given a job. The first obstacle had been overcome. Thereafter, for several hours each morning. Storey worked in the garden. He planted peas and beans, and he tended them meticulously. But we had no outside contact yet who could get us the things we needed.

They eventually found their contact in a fellow-prisoner, a murderer called Jenkins, who was due for release shortly.

During the next two months Woolley, Storey and I were three model prisoners. We were like kids before Christmas, during those two long months. We were working out a plan and the more we pondered over it the better we liked it. Meanwhile we didn't want to attract any undue attention to ourselves. We saw as much of Jenkins as we could. We had every confidence that he would do his part when the time came. He wouldn't do it out of friendship for us or hatred for the Japs, he'd do it as a matter of business. Jenkins was obviously the kind of man who would rather earn a dishonest penny than an honest dollar. Over and over again, we told him what we expected him to do. He was to go to a friend of mine in Shanghai, get what we wanted, and then toss the blades over the wall. We drew a map of Chusan Road and showed him where to stand when he threw the blades over. With luck, they would clear the twenty-five foot wall and drop among Storey's beans.

We had entered Ward Road Prison 8th June, 1942. Now it was September, 1944. We had been there twenty-seven months. All of us had lost considerable weight, but Woolley, Storey and I were in fair condition. Mori was not a bad jailer. He was a weak, vacillating man, susceptible to flattery and kumshaw. I hinted to him that I had friends outside who could get us some food and that I would gladly share it with him. Mori accepted my kindness. The escape would put a severe strain on us physically, and we wanted to be in as good condition as possible when the time came. Our bodies desperately needed some reserve of fat for the gruelling job ahead of us. We were all right for one sharp, concentrated effort, but we would probably have to walk between 600 and 700 miles (assuming we got out of Shanghai), and it was this prospect that worried us. With Mori's connivance, I sent messages to friends outside and they didn't fail me. Soon a supply of canned stuff began to arrive. The sausages, peanut butter and sugar looked beautiful when we opened the tins. Mori, of course, got his share. This extra food helped Woolley and Storey a great deal. It came a little too late to help me, unfortunately.

There was a slight ledge which ran along the wall of my cell. It was about six inches from the floor. I could just get a toehold on it and reach my barred window. When the blades arrived I would have to spend many hours standing on that precarious ledge reaching upward to the bar. I began to practise balancing on that narrow ledge, hanging on to one bar with my left hand and holding my right hand aloft. It was a very uncomfortable position. Little-used muscles were brought into play. In the upward stretch the abdominal muscles became involved as well as the back muscles of the legs. My leg muscles were fine, but one day, as I reached up toward the bars, I felt something snap. An excruciating pain shot through my lower abdomen and I doubled up.

I slipped off my trousers and investigated. There was a sharp bulge above my groin on both sides. I knew what had happened, all right. It was a double rupture. I had seen this often enough at sea but never thought I'd become a victim. I knew the reason, and afterwards doctors confirmed my diagnosis. The intestines are held in position by a wall that keeps them where they belong. This wall is made up of fat and muscle. Usually it's a tough, durable wall, but if you've been badly fed for a couple of years the fat thins out. In my case there was no fat and only a thin wall. Merely the strain of reaching up with my arm had punctured that wall and part of my viscera had dropped through it.

I sat on the edge of my cot, thoroughly discouraged for the first time since 7th December. This meant the end of everything. Now I'd probably rot in prison until the war was over. I let my hand slide over the bulge in my side. Curiously, the pain was gone, even under pressure. Standing up, I investigated further. I discovered that if I pressed the bulge on the right side it didn't bother me, the breakthrough on the left side wasn't so bad. I tried a few steps. As long as I held my right hand against my sagging abdomen, pressing it back tightly, there was practically no pain. I didn't sleep much that night, trying to figure things out. Suppose I went to the Chinese doctors in the prison and asked them to operate. If you've been a ship's captain for as many years as I have, you learn quite a bit about rudimentary surgery. It would be a simple enough operation, and the Chinese doctors would probably do a good job. They'd just have to put my viscera back in place and sew up the hole in the peritoneal wall. But what was there to sew up? There wasn't enough tissue to hold stitches. Muscle alone couldn't do it. Then, too, I was in no condition for an operation. Oh, I felt all right, but I was feeling with my mind these days. Considering my body objectively, as a surgeon might, I came to the conclusion that it was in no condition to weather an operation successfully. I wouldn't die, but the operation would leave me so weak that it would take weeks, if not months, to recover my strength. I decided to forget the whole business of doctors.

Now came another question. Woolley and I had agreed that a three-man team would have the best chance of making a break. Any more than that would be an unwieldy unit. A two-man team would be all right, unless one of the team was killed. It would be tough making it alone. All in all, looking at it from every angle, we had decided that three made the perfect escape team. But now, with me able to walk only when I supported my rupture, would I be able to pull my weight with my two partners? They didn't need my strength. Storey had the youth, the vitality, the strength. They didn't need my courage. Woolley had enough raw courage for a division. But they needed my tongue. It would be suicidal to walk across 600 or 700 miles of country occupied by Japs and puppet Chinese, unless you knew Chinese well and some Japanese. The rupture hadn't deprived me of my tongue. Not that I could have translated the poetry of Li Po or the philosophy of Mencius in flowery Cantonese, but I did know my way around Mandarin dialect, which is the everyday language of about 300 million people in Northern, Western and South-western China. My Japanese would never have fooled Lafcadio Hearn or Tojo, but I knew enough of it to pass as a French priest, or to know what to do if a Nip sentry yelled, 'Halt or I'll shoot!' Neither Storey nor Woolley knew Chinese or Japanese. Of course, I could back out and get them a substitute, but who in hell would I get? Thinking over the list of our fellow prisoners, I didn't know of one who was familiar enough with the languages and customs to guide Woolley and Storey. So I decided to sleep on it. I've always found that to be a good idea. I dreamed that night of Rita. When I woke in the morning all my doubts were dissipated. I'd go along, rupture or no rupture. I'd go along on one leg and trust to the strength of Woolley and Storey to carry me.

I told Woolley about my accident.

'I'd never think about trying it without you, Smitty,' he said in surprise when I told him of the doubts I had. 'Hell, man, Storey and I would be nabbed before we reached Chaou Foong Road. It isn't your stomach we need, Smitty man, it's your brains and your knowledge of this Godforsaken country.'

'I'm apt to be a hell of a burden to you and Storey,' I said, still a bit on the fence, but wanting terribly to be convinced.

'Storey is a marine, isn't he?' Woolley asked. 'I hear great tales of your marines. If things get bad, man, he can carry you.' Which was, of course, impossible.

I felt confident now that we'd pull it off. Perhaps Woolley's faith was all I needed to give me that extra bit of confidence. I decided to write my brother Linton and tell him my plans. He would tell Rita and at least she'd know that I wasn't just rotting away in jail. I had such supreme contempt for the Japanese Intelligence that I didn't worry about revealing my plans in a letter to my doctor brother.

About a month later he received the letter in Atlanta. One line caught his eye, and he understood, as I knew he would. 'A continuous stretch, further than from your house to Sam's' meant a lot to my brother. We had only one mutual friend named Sam. That was Judge Samuel J. Murphy of Bradentown, Florida. I knew that Linton would figure out that it was a little more than 600 miles from Atlanta to Sam's house in Bradentown. Six hundred miles? Six hundred miles from Shanghai would mean freedom. My brother studied the letter which, incidentally, was passed without a cut by the stupid censor, and immediately phoned Rita to say I was escaping soon and would walk to freedom.

Woolley left the planning to me. I knew Shanghai well, of course. I knew every road of it (there are no 'streets' in Shanghai), and I knew the surrounding country. To refresh my memory, I had smuggled a handy little book out of the prison library. It was called *Shanghai Dialect in Four Weeks* and it was written by two gentlemen named Charles Ho and George Fo. Whether or not anyone could learn Shanghai dialect in four weeks (or four years) is not the point. The point is that the little blue book contained an excellent map of Shanghai. I pored over it in my cell. Assuming we did get over the wall, which way would we go? First we'd have to get out of the city. If we went due north, we'd find ourselves in open country within a mile. If we turned to the right or east, we'd find the Whangpu River, which was well guarded. If we turned to the left (south-west), we had damn near the whole city of Shanghai to walk through before we found open country. For various reasons we decided to take what appeared the greater risk. There were plenty of ack-ack batteries to the east and north, and these were restricted areas where we would need all sorts of military passes. There were main highways, well patrolled, and railroads, well guarded, and the more I thought of the prospect of taking what on the map looked the easier way, the more I doubted it. Then, too, once we had escaped from the jail the Japanese would immediately think we had headed for the north, or the east, and they'd go over the flat terrain with fine combs. No one would think we'd have the audacity to walk right through the city proper. No one would think we'd attempt to walk across such well-lighted thoroughfares as Broadway or the Bund. They'd never think we'd have the bad judgement to cross the Garden Bridge over Suchow Creek and amble through the French Settlement and then head west across the tracks of the Hangchow Railway and over the Chung San Road and into the plains and hills beyond. That was doing it the hard way. In many ways it was leading to our opponents' strength, but many a grand slam has been made at bridge that way and we had to make a grand slam. A little slam wouldn't help us in this game. It was all or nothing.

Woolley, Storey and I agreed on the route we would take. We memorised it road by road. Once we got out we'd do as little talking as possible. We'd have everything memorised. I wrote the route down on paper and gave Woolley and Storey each a copy to learn. They learned the names of the roads and two or three rendezvous where we'd meet in case of any unexpected separation. Then they destroyed the papers.

Then one morning, while taking our exercise (it was just a week since Jenkins had been released), I saw Storey straighten up. I saw him take a piece of burlap from a pole and drop it casually among the beans. Then he turned and looked toward me. He nodded slightly and went back to his beans. Jenkins had come through. I felt icily calm and, to my surprise, not a bit excited. Subconsciously I had banked completely on Jenkins. I had a strong conviction that the murderer would not fail us. Now, at least, we had a chance.

We went back into the cell block. We always had a few minutes of rather informal milling about in the corridors. The Jap guards were so accustomed to us now, and to our apparently resigned behaviour, that their supervision was slack. Storey slipped me a small package, which he had secreted down his trouser leg. I hurried to my cell. Woolley leaned against the bars of his cell, ready to warn me if a guard came down the corridor. I opened the package. There were four blades – long, slender, ten-inch blades. I looked dubiously at the bars across the window. They were three-quarter-inch hardened steel. Would these frail-looking blades be able to cut through one of these bars? I took one and buried the others in a secret place I had prepared. I moved my stool to the window. I couldn't use the ledge very comfortably now. One hand had to support my abdomen and the other had to handle the blade. I stood on the three-legged stool and drew the file across the lower right-hand bar. There were four vertical and two horizontal bars across the window. Months before I had calculated that if I could remove the lower section of the vertical bar to the right, it would leave a space of eight and five-eighths inches by fourteen and three-quarters. This would be a tight squeeze, but by pushing the head and then both shoulders through I thought the rest of one's body could make it. The blade cut slowly but surely into the steel. I looked back at Woolley across the corridor and waved a reassuring hand to him. I intended to saw through the bar in two places, where it was imbedded in the concrete of the window ledge and eight and five-eighths inches above that, where it joined the lower horizontal bar. It would take some time to do this, but time was the cheapest commodity in Ward Road Jail. I had already hidden a small bar of soap and some shoe blacking I had stolen. Once the bar was cut, I'd fill the space with soap and then blacken it. This would defy a casual inspection, and for months the Japs hadn't given us anything but casual inspections. I worked as long as I could, which was about an hour. Then my wrist muscles rebelled, I had to give up.

Every night I worked for at least an hour on that stubborn steel. The blade was a beautiful thing. Its sharp little teeth never dulled or blunted. Meanwhile, I had broken the blades in half and distributed one piece to Woolley, one to Storey, and one to each of Commander Cunningham's men.* They were to do nothing until I had filed through the bar across my window. All of us would escape through that one space. Meanwhile, there were other things to be done. We were all gathering as many scraps of cloth and clothing as we could find. On the big night each of us would make a dummy to leave in our beds. The Jap guards were creatures of habit. One of them walked down the corridor every hour on the hour. Believing us to be thoroughly cowed, the guards never bothered to do more than glance into our cells.

I continued sawing. The steel seemed to get harder as I cut through it, but it gave. After three weeks I heard a little click and my blade came right through. The bottom half of the bar was separated from its concrete foundation. Now I went to work on the top of the bar. I had to reach up for that, which wasn't pleasant, but now I was buoyed up by a hope that was tangible. It wasn't just a dream any more. I was actually doing something. I was on my way, and sharp streaks of pain in my abdomen were only minor annoyances. A week or two more and the bar hung by a shred. Three or four minutes with the blade and it, too, would be free. I carefully soaped the scars and blackened the soap.

We would make the attempt in three days. I sent out word to my friend to contact Jenkins and gave him the date. The escape would have to be accomplished in perfect silence. If the night was still, a whisper might carry to a Jap guard. The sensible thing was to give orders now. I wrote out a set of plans for Woolley, Storey and Commander Cunningham. The men would go out of

* *Commander Cunningham had heard of their escape plan and wanted to join the break with his own group of escapers. The two parties were to climb out together but split up as soon as they reached the roadway.*

the window in order. I studied the opening carefully. First you had to put your left foot on the small ledge. Then your right foot on the three-legged stool, being careful not to knock it over. Your right arm would grasp the lower horizontal bar across the window. You would pull yourself up, resting the right knee on the window ledge, as you stuck your head through the opening. Your left hand would grasp the knotted sheets. . . . I went on like that. Every detail was engraved in my mind. No man would have to do any independent thinking until we reached the street. He would only have to remember, 'Now with my right hand I grab the rope, and then with my left hand, etc., etc. . . .' I went over the written plan with Woolley and Commander Cunningham and in general we agreed. Cunningham did not like the method I had planned to get us atop the twenty-five-foot wall. He had another method he liked better.

I had a fourth copy of the plan which I kept in my pocket. I gave the men the word to start cutting through the door bars. Each cell was guarded by a door or gate which had four upright bars and one horizontal bar. They were five-eighths-inch steel. The horizontal bar was midway across the gate. My idea was that each one of us should saw through one of the lower sections of one of the vertical bars right where it joined the horizontal or cross-bar. The bar could then be bent back, the men could slip through the opening into the corridor, bend the bar back to its normal position, fill the small opening with soap and blacking, and come to my cell. We would all escape from my cell. We all worked on the cell-door bars during the night of 5th October. We sawed from the inside, getting the job three-quarters done. The next night, when the guard finished his usual 2100 (9 p.m.) round, the men would all hurriedly finish cutting the bar, prepare a decoy, escape, then replace the bar. Then they would hurry to my cell, entering it through the opening I would have made in my door. Each man would bring a sheet with him.

It was while finishing this last cutting job that the first of an incredibly lucky chain of incidents happened – lucky in their outcome. The jail was in pitch darkness, as conservation of electricity was the order of the day for all of Shanghai, and the jail was encompassed in deathly silence. I was sawing away at the door bar as noiselessly as possible by sense of touch, while Woolley, from across the corridor, and I both kept watch as closely as possible in the inky blackness. I had paused momentarily to rest weary fingers and to listen, when suddenly a light flared into my startled face from not more than three or four feet away. A harsh and threatening bark, such as only Huns and Japs make when aroused, rang in my ears. It was Mori, the superintendent of the jail, making a surprise inspection. He was wearing rubber-soled shoes, and had walked right up to me without either Woolley or myself hearing him. I thrust the bit of hacksaw blade into my pockets as unobtrusively as possible and with what must have been a trembling voice asked what was wrong. With the light still steadily burning in my eyes, he said, 'What is that light burning for?' Just to the right of my cell was the hangman's room, which had a wooden door – a one-way door, so to speak. Someone had turned on the light inside the space during the day and had forgotten to switch it off, and now a thin and barely visible rim of light framed the door. I explained to him what had probably happened, and that the switch was inside the locked door. He grunted and walked off. I don't know how Woolley felt, but the cold sweat rolled off me in streams, and I felt weak. If he had canted the light downward just a tiny bit, even a Jap would have seen the blade and would have grasped the situation.

The day of 6th October dawned. It was a chilly day, a bit overcast, which was fine. We didn't want too much

moon that night. It was a long day, the longest I have
ever spent. About noon I reached into my pocket to get
the list of my detailed plan. I wanted to go over it just
once more to make sure I had left nothing undone. I put
my hand into my pocket and then froze with horror.
The pockets were empty. My hands began to sweat. I
tried to think. I knew I'd put that plan in my back right-
hand pocket two days before. Two days before? Then I
remembered a guard throwing in a clean suit to me and
telling me to throw out the suit I was wearing. It was to
be washed. I had stripped it off and tossed it through
the bars. I had tossed it through the bars, and perhaps
tossed my head with it. I remembered with horror the
things I had written. 'Storey will climb the rope to the
watchtower first, followed by Smith and Woolley.' My
head? Woolley and Storey, too, would lose their heads.
That suit with its precious plan was now in the laundry
down below. Did they empty the pockets when they
washed clothes? Probably. The Japs were always looking
for anything that was in writing. The afternoon wore on.
I expected to hear the sharp clump of heavy feet on the
steel corridor floor any minute. Woolley, calm as always,
started talking across to me, but I couldn't answer him.
I didn't tell him of the horrible mistake I had made – a
mistake that might prove fatal to all of us. I reproached
myself bitterly. 'They've been depending on your
brains,' I said over and over again to myself. 'You let
them down, you fool!'

It was chilly that afternoon, but I sat there on my cot
bathed in sweat.

The afternoon wore on somehow and we had our
evening meal. Our last supper was as tasteless and scanty
as usual. I finally shook off the mood I was in and just
assumed they'd never find that plan of mine. After dinner
there was nothing to do but wait. It seemed as though the
whole prison was waiting. You could feel the tenseness

and expectancy in the air. I am convinced that every man in that jail knew we were going to try to make the break that night. You can't keep secrets in a prison. As the evening wore on the quiet became more intense. Usually we whispered across the corridors to men in opposite cells, or we talked to the men in cells on either side of us. Not tonight. I kept looking at my watch. Strangely, the Japs had never taken my watch. I took inventory of what I had in my pockets. I had a watch, two snapshots of Rita and some stolen paper and a pencil. That was all. We couldn't, of course, take any food with us. We didn't have a weapon or a compass among the eight of us. If we ever did get clear and if it ever came to a showdown we'd have to depend on the good right arms of Storey and Woolley. I relaxed, thinking of those two grand men. Even if we were caught and did get the axe, well, I couldn't have picked two better men to die with. You knew they'd die well; Storey calmly, looking disdainfully at his executioners; Woolley with dignity and courage.

And now it was 2100 (9 p.m.). Far down the corridor I could hear the steps of the guard. He was always on time. He had made his rounds on the tier above. He would walk the length of my corridor, then descend a flight of steps to the big rotunda, and if he followed normal procedure, he'd sit in a chair and take a nap. Ward Road Jail was so secure, so completely escape-proof, that the Japs felt they didn't need many guards at night, once the place was locked up. The steps came closer. He was sauntering along slowly. I wished he would quicken his steps. I didn't want his glance to dwell too long on any of the bars. He might spot the blackened soap. But he didn't. He kept on, reached the end of the corridor, and then started down. Before his steps had died away I had my blade out. It scraped across the last sliver of steel that held the bar in place. I worked fast now. Removing one

sheet and one blanket from my bed, I fixed the scraps of
burlap and cloth into the form of a dummy and placed
it under the blanket on the bed. Seven other men were
doing the same thing, yet I couldn't hear a sound.
Woolley had secured his bar in place, filled the crack
with soap and then blackened it. He came across the corridor and stuck his handsome face through the space left
by the bar I had sawed through. He stepped into my
cell. Storey arrived a moment later. We didn't utter a
word. I took two sheets from each of them and knotted
the six sheets together. The day before, Storey had smuggled in a strong two-foot length of bamboo from his
garden. I tied the end of my sheet-rope to the middle of
that. My idea was to catch the strong piece of bamboo
between two of the bars and then let the knotted sheets
drop down on the outside. The bamboo would be horizontal; the sheet vertical. The bamboo was what we call
in ships a 'toggle'.

Woolley gave me a boost to the ledge of the window.
I pulled out the bar and that left a space slightly under
nine by fifteen inches. The last man out would replace
the bar in the cell door and bar the window, soap the
cracks and blacken them.

I adjusted my bamboo toggle so that it fitted between
the two vertical bars above our escape space. The knotted sheets dangled below. There was a drop of twenty-
two feet to the concrete walk below. I had measured this
with my eye. I had measured it every time I went into
the courtyard to exercise. I had measured it perhaps 600
times and came to the conclusion that it was twenty-two
feet, give or take three or four inches. The knotted sheets
were twenty-two feet long. If the knots held, we'd at
least get into the courtyard. Automatically I stuck my
head and right arm through the space, hunched my
right shoulder through, then my left foot. I reached up
and grabbed the top knot of the sheet. I swung my body

and my legs out into space, forgetting about a red-hot
iron that was lying just above my groin. Glancing back,
I saw Commander Cunningham and his men entering
the cell. I swung down. The 'rope' swayed back and forth
a little, but I didn't worry about that. I weighed 190
pounds on 8th December, 1941. I was about 120 now.
Hand over hand I slipped down the knotted sheets and
then my feet hit the concrete. It was dark and there was
a chill wind blowing. The moon wasn't very high yet,
not bright enough to give much light.

I hadn't taken a step away from the rope when
Woolley's feet hit the concrete. Then one of Commander
Cunningham's men followed. Storey was next, and now,
according to plan, he ran to his garden and picked up
two long strips of bamboo he had constructed by lashing
the two-foot pieces together for the ostensible purpose of
having a climbing frame for his beans. We crept across
the courtyard, feeling naked, somehow, and very conspicuous. Woolley was carrying our rope of knotted
sheets. Cunningham and his men were using their own.
There was a watchtower at the corner where the walls
intersected. A man stood guard there all day, but he
went off duty at nine o'clock. Storey and Woolley
attached the bamboo toggle to the long bamboo pole
and reached it twenty-five feet above to the bars of the
watchtower. They had to insert the toggle behind and
between two bars, so that it would hold firmly. The long
bamboo stretcher bent and swayed in the wind. We held
our breath, afraid that it might break, but although
bamboo is flexible it doesn't break easily. Finally, the
toggle caught and we pulled the rope taut. It held nicely.
Storey, the youngest and strongest, scaled up first. He
went up that sheet, hand over hand, like a real sailor.
When he neared the top, he grabbed the bars of the
watchtower and pulled himself up to the little four-inch
coping that jutted out below the bars. I went up next

and almost fell back at the halfway mark. I was weaker than I thought. I hitched my legs around the knotted sheets, secured what purchase I could with my feet on the knots, and pulled and pushed myself up. Another knot – one more knot – and then Storey's strong arm reached down, he gave a tug, and I was up beside him. Woolley came up, and then, again according to plan, Commander Cunningham's man followed. Cunningham hadn't liked our method of reaching the tower atop the wall. He had contrived another method with a different kind of rope made of sheets and blankets. That's why his man came up via our rope, so that he could help secure Cunningham's rope to the bars of the watchtower. Edging over toward the wall, I looked down into the street. The watchtower was semi-circular, and as long as we didn't step on to the top of the wall itself there was little possibility that we would be seen. Less than twenty feet from the tower, that is, from the street intersection, a brilliant street light blazed.

I prayed for an air-raid alarm. It would mean blacking out the streets, but the air force was somewhere else that night. The street was crowded with Europeans, Chinese and Japs. They were mostly shopkeepers on their way home. Jap soldiers sauntered by. We couldn't drop down among that crowd without being noticed. We waited, hoping in vain for the streets to clear. The moon rose higher, and it hung like a beacon in the still, dark sky. It was the brightest moon I had ever seen. Commander Cunningham's group was having trouble with their rope. They couldn't raise it up to the tower. It was dangerous to wait any longer. We had been hanging to the outside of the tower half an hour now. We might as well make a break for it, then Commander Cunningham and his men could use our rope and toggle. I fixed our rope between two bars of the watchtower and then threw the knotted sheets over the wall. The end of the sheet hadn't straightened out before I was sliding down the rope, not bothering to slow my descent. My feet touched the ground and Woolley's feet were almost on my head. There were gasps of astonishment from people on the street. They stopped and looked, but no one did anything. Storey was over the wall now, and Cunningham's man was hauling up the rope so that his group could use it. I started to walk rapidly toward the right. I walked diagonally across the street, Woolley to the left and Storey went straight across. We kept our heads lowered and affected an unconcern we didn't feel. I expected someone's hand to clamp down on my shoulder any minute, but meanwhile I was gaining. Every yard away from the prison wall meant a yard nearer safety. By now, Commander Cunningham and his men should be dropping over the wall, but they weren't crossing the street; they were heading east then north along the Kwen Ning Road. I was across the street and walking along the dimly-lit Chusan Road. I walked a block to reach the intersection of Chusan and Tong Shan. Jenkins should be waiting here. He should be standing in the shadows on the north-east corner. He should have coolie clothes for us to slip over our grey prison garb. He should have money and food and papers. If he would be there, I felt that everything would be all right. I stopped and waited at the north-east corner. Woolley and Storey had circled and joined me. We hadn't said a word yet. There was no outcry from the prison, a block behind. That augured well. It meant Cunningham and his group* had got away too. The three of us waited for Jenkins to walk out of the shadows. But there were no shadows; the moonlight had penetrated that dark corner. And there was no Jenkins. We waited thirty seconds – one minute – no Jenkins. We dared not wait any longer. We had to put space between us and the

* *Later recaptured.*

prison. It was 10.35 p.m. Jenkins was to have been there at ten o'clock. He was thirty-five minutes late. Jenkins had failed us.

'We'd better go on,' I said. They both nodded. We didn't need many words between us. Of course, we had considered the possibility of Jenkins not appearing. If he didn't show up, we had planned to go to my friend's house. We walked along Tong Shan Road, a dimly lit street of ramshackle shops and miserable houses. We slouched along, trying to look like three tired men on the way home after a hard day's work. We circled and struck to the left, toward the river, at Chaou Foong Road. We reached Broadway (the waterfront docks) and turned right. Ahead and across the street, I saw a file of Chinese police. They stood at the entrance of the Garden Bridge, which we'd have to cross. They were stopping people at the entrance to the bridge and asking for papers. But they were on the other side of the street. We kept walking in silence. We stepped on to the bridge and kept going. All the traffic was against us. Automobiles and horsedrawn carts in the middle and people walking on the small passages on either side. The bridge is only about 100 yards across but it seemed like miles. Toward the end of the bridge, I looked up and saw a group of Jap soldiers standing at the opposite end. Their backs were to us, and I noticed that they were asking for identification papers from people coming on the bridge. We walked on, right past the Jap soldiers, who apparently thought our papers had been looked at by the Chinese police at the other end. We walked past them and mingled with the crowd on the Bund and then Nanking Road. The back of my neck was covered with sweat, but I felt strangely exhilarated. We were free! Sure, it might be only a minute or an hour more, but at least for the moment it was a nice feeling.

The three men headed west out of Shanghai, hoping to meet up with Chinese guerrillas. With the brave and generous help of Chinese peasants and farmers they struggled on. Smith's legs were black with broken blood vessels and the toenails came away from Woolley's feet. They made contact with Chinese Nationalist soldiers on 11th October and were led across country to the Nationalist Headquarters where they rested before travelling on towards Chungking, beyond the Japanese lines and through a pocket held by the Chinese Army, into Japanese-occupied territory once more. They reached a secret American field hospital where they rested before trekking on for another six days to an emergency airfield, 700 miles from Shanghai. They were flown across Japanese-held territory to Kunming, then on to Calcutta where an old friend greeted them with the news that they were officially dead and must keep under cover. 'The Japs announced your capture and execution some time ago.' On 30th November they had a celebration dinner for three in Calcutta; then Woolley [subsequently awarded the O.B.E.] *was sent to Ceylon to report to Lord Mountbatten, and Smith and Storey were flown to Washington. After reporting to Admiral Nimitz in Guam, and being given a bird's eye view of the American fleet at sea – his one desire – Smith was flown home to San Francisco, still officially dead. He went straight to his wife's apartment. 'I rang the bell and then Rita opened the door, and the long 4½ years of separation were as though they'd never been. Now I was home.'*

17

The Escapes of Oberleutnant Franz von Werra of the Luftwaffe, from Swanwick P.O.W. Camp near Derby in England, and from a transit train in Canada, 20th December, 1940 and 25th January, 1941

This account of the escapes of Oberleutnant Franz von Werra, subsequently promoted to Hauptmann and awarded the Knight's Insignia of the Iron Cross, is taken from Single or Return, *by his fellow-prisoner Kapitänleutnant (later Korvetten-kapitän) Fritz Wentzel.*

Wentzel was captured on 30th October, 1940, when U.32, the submarine aboard which he was serving, was depth-charged in the Atlantic by H.M.S. Harvester. *He was sent to the prison camp at Swanwick near Derby. The nephew of Gunther Pluschow, a German officer who had escaped successfully from England during World War I, he felt he had a certain family tradition to live up to, and became involved in escape plans. He was not, however, one of the five officers who broke out of Swanwick through a tunnel on 20th December, 1940. Oberleutnant Wagner and Oberleutnant Wilhelm went as one pair, Oberleutnant Mannhardt and Kapitän Cramer as the other; both pairs were shortly recaptured. Lieutenant von Werra* [who had previously escaped from Grizedale Hall but been recaptured] *went alone:*

Lieutenant Franz von Werra was the first man through the tunnel. As he had been the leading spirit in the whole undertaking so he had done most of the work and it was he who made the final break through. At the end there was only a relatively thin layer of earth still left and if by bad luck a guard had happened to go that way and tread on that particular patch of earth it would certainly have caved in. But fortunately the path between the two gardens was rarely if ever used.

It was 20th December and the evening roll-call was over by 8.30. The five escapers and their helpers went straight to the corner room where the tunnel began under the floor and without wasting time they got to work. Von Werra put on his 'Dutch' flying kit and over that he wore the digging clothes that he had been using for the past six weeks every day on the tunnelling. In the meantime the others had opened up the hole and switched the light on. They all shook hands silently and rather hurriedly and von Werra lowered himself into the pit.

'Good luck!' he heard as he got down to enter the tunnel proper. 'I shall need it,' he thought. The tunnel was very narrow and he could go forward only on his elbows. It was the sort of progress he had learnt on the barrack square. How often had he cursed it? But it stood him in good stead now. When he reached the vertical shaft he could almost stand upright. 'Light out!' he called through the air-pipe, which also served as a breathing tube. The light went out and he set to work.

That was at about nine o'clock. Fresh, damp autumnal earth fell down on to his head and shoulders but he had put a covering on his head and he wore airman's goggles to protect his eyes so that didn't matter. The bottom of the exit pit was rather lower than the tunnel so there was no need to carry away the earth that was falling now; he just stamped it in with his feet as he worked.

Von Werra was working with a large spoon and from

time to time he dug it carefully upwards to see if he was through. After about ten minutes' hard work the great moment came, the spoon went through. Now he took a square piece of board, put it on his head and pressed gradually but powerfully upwards at the same time using a knife to cut round the edges. The top layer gave way and the opening was free. Carefully he put the earth-covered board, which was to be used as a cover, to one side – the last man would need it to cover up the hole.

Von Werra had already cut himself a few steps in the pit and with their aid he easily clambered out of it. The moon was not yet up and it was still dark. He could see enough to make out that the hole was where it was supposed to be, between the fences of the two neglected gardens. A little distance away he could make out the dark shape of our dormitory. It was perfectly blacked out. The guards saw to that every night. They took great care to see that no German bombs fell on us.

From where he was von Werra could not see the watch-tower, which was just as well because it meant that the sentry in the watch-tower couldn't see him – not even if he used his searchlight. Everything had really gone according to plan. So much so, in fact, that there was no need for any special precautions. There was, for example, no need for him to be quiet, for the choir was making such a noise that footsteps or anything else would never be heard. On the other hand, there was no reason to lose any time so he set off on his own as arranged, bending double as he moved along the right-hand fence. Then he looked round. He could just see the top of the nearest watch-tower now. If he kept well down the sentry would be unable to see him.

He had to climb over two fences before he reached a narrow roadway. On one side were a number of houses. He didn't know whether they were occupied or not;

they certainly looked as though they were deserted, but that may have been just the blackout. There were no houses on the other side of the road, but the fields were not open to the roadway as they usually are in Germany. These were separated by a wall which von Werra now climbed. On the other side was meadowland, which was good, for he didn't want to use the roads yet. The other escapers would not be particularly obvious in their civilian clothing and they would mingle easily with other people but von Werra in his supposed Dutch uniform wanted to stay out of sight as long as possible. He therefore went along behind the wall, making in a southerly direction. Every hundred yards or so he came to a transverse wall and this had to be climbed, but the walls were not very high and it was easy enough. Not all the fields were grassland, some of them were under the plough, but nevertheless he made fair progress. Whenever he heard a car or a pedestrian on the other side of the wall he stopped dead to let them pass before venturing on.

He had looked at his watch when he first climbed out of the tunnel. The illuminated dial had shown it to be exactly 9.15. It was one o'clock now. He had been tramping for almost four hours. Then ahead of him he saw a small group of houses which he decided to bypass, but first of all he thought he'd take a rest and he found a convenient haystack. He would have loved a cigarette, but he did not dare light up.

After an hour's rest he got on his way again, making a wide detour round the village until he reached the road again. This time he used it. He was a good way from the camp now and his plans demanded that he should now show himself. In fact he was waiting to fall in with someone, whereupon he would exclaim in his supposedly Dutch English:

'Isn't there a telephone around here anywhere a

fellow can use? I've had to make a forced landing and I've been tramping around for over an hour. I must get hold of a telephone.'

But he tramped on and on and fell in with no one to whom he could complain bitterly about the dearth of telephones. Left completely to his own devices the Luftwaffe Lieutenant Franz von Werra wandered disconsolately through the hostile but sleeping English countryside. This must have gone on for another couple of hours and then he came to a rather larger inhabited centre. If he didn't meet anyone he'd have to knock someone up. There'd be a telephone around somewhere from which he could phone up the nearest air-field.

He had another look at his watch. Four o'clock. Small wonder there were so few people on the roads. Would it be better perhaps to wait until it grew light? He decided to wait and after a little search he found a barn and in this he took shelter. He wasn't afraid to light a cigarette now; it would make no difference to his plans if it betrayed his presence there – he would just tell his story that much earlier; that was all.

Just before six von Werra walked in the direction of the town. The very first house, which lay in the surrounding country, seemed to be a farm to judge by its adjacent buildings. He went up to the front door boldly and knocked. He could hear that people were already about. A woman opened the door and stared at the strange visitor in astonishment.

'I am a Dutch airman,' he declared. 'I had to make a forced landing in the neighbourhood and I must get into touch with the nearest airfield. Can you direct me there?'

'Come in. I'll ask my husband. Are you hurt?'

'Fortunately, no,' answered von Werra. 'Rather dirty, that's all.'

Believing him to be Dutch and an ally the woman was

very willing to help. She gave him a cup of tea and said that the men would be back from milking in a few minutes.

Werra talked to her all the time while he was waiting, anxious to give his story an airing. He told her about his mother, whom he hadn't seen for a year – and she was duly sympathetic – he told her about his escape from Holland to England and about his bombing raids on Germany. She lapped it up.

In a few minutes the husband arrived and he was as surprised as his wife but just as eager to be helpful. He told him that Hucknall was the nearest airfield, but von Werra felt his heart sink on being told their telephone was out of order. He was, however, given careful directions to the call-box at Condor Park station.

'I must get along,' he said. 'Thank you very much for your assistance.' 'It went on wheels,' he thought elatedly. 'They'll swallow it just as well at the airfield.'

After half-an-hour's walk he was inside the call-box and on the line to Hucknall aerodrome.

'Give me the Duty Officer please,' demanded von Werra when he got through. And when he was put through to that officer he said confidently: 'Captain van Lott of the Royal Dutch Air Force here. My Wellington was damaged over Denmark in the night. I tried to get her back but I didn't quite make it. The others baled out – they must be around somewhere – and I made a belly landing. Send along a car for me, will you? I can let you know the rest at the airfield.'

'Where are you now?' came the question.

'Condor Park Station,' said von Werra.

'The car will be there in twenty minutes.'

Outside the station an R.A.F. corporal opened the door of the car for him. He acknowledged the man's salute shortly as he had seen British officers do, and got in.

The corporal sat in front with the driver and there was

no need to say anything further. In ten minutes they were at the airfield. The car was driven right up to the main entrance to the administrative building and once again the R.A.F. corporal opened the car door and saluted.

Von Werra went up the steps. The Duty Officer was already there to greet him.

'Can I speak to the Adjutant?' he asked at once. He realised that at this early hour – it wasn't yet seven – it was very unlikely that the Commandant himself would be around.

'The Adjutant's in the picture,' replied the officer. 'He'll be along in a minute. I expect you'd like some breakfast?'

'Don't want to spare the time,' returned von Werra. 'I want a machine to get back to my base as quickly as possible.'

'The Adjutant'll attend to that. You'll have time enough for eggs and bacon,' and he led von Werra into the mess.

'Hallo!' shouted a number of flying types already attending to their breakfasts. 'Take a pew, Dutchie.'

Von Werra almost clicked his heels together, bowed shortly and said 'Von Werra!' – but not quite. The sort of thing that comes as second nature to a German is just the thing to be on your guard against, and he was.

'Had a spot of bother, what? Other chaps all right?'

'Probably,' replied von Werra. He was in the thick of it now.

'What were you flying, a Whitley?'

'No, a Wellington.'

'Not bad old kites. Where were you?'

'Over Denmark. Plenty of ack-ack and night fighters. Anyhow what I must do is to call up my own base right away.' He was shown to a telephone and began talking into the instrument with the deceptive naturalness of a skilled actor. In fact he did not even call the exchange.

Then the Adjutant arrived and he had to tell his story all over again – and in detail this time. No one seemed suspicious. No one seemed to find anything odd about his uniform. No one seemed to find his broken Dutch English anything but normal. In any case, there were all sorts of foreign airmen in England on service: Dutch, French, Norwegians . . .

But then came the moment when von Werra asked for a plane.

'We haven't one to spare at the moment,' said the Adjutant, and von Werra thought he was hesitant.

Now they casually began to mention dangerous things: von Werra's supposed squadron; his base. He began to feel a little uncomfortable. That sort of thing could floor him quicker than anything else. He must do his best not to get involved in anything but a general discussion. He extricated himself from the difficulty for the moment by going to the lavatory. 'They'll start asking about names in a minute,' he thought anxiously. Had anyone noticed anything? He thought not so far though the Adjutant had looked at him a bit strangely – but even that could have been his imagination. He'd never be able to get through all the questioning so perhaps the best thing would be if he had a look round to see if he could find a machine on his own. He climbed out of the lavatory window and carefully reconnoitred the position of the runways.

Airfields are much the same all over the world and this one wasn't much different. But from the type of the majority of the planes he could see it seemed to him that it must be a training-station, and it was nearly three-quarters of an hour since leaving the mess before he found a Hurricane with a mechanic refuelling it.

'Nice job, these Hurricanes.'

'This one's due for a major,' replied the mechanic

innocently. 'Going back to the works to-day.'

'Thought I was right,' said von Werra with a sudden stroke of genius. 'I'm the pilot come to take her.'

'Strike a light!' said the man admiringly, 'that's quick work. Hang on. I'll get the papers.'

'Oh, never mind about the papers,' said von Werra. 'Let's get going.'

'Can't do anything without papers,' said the mechanic firmly. 'There's a war on,' and off he went.

Not in too great a hurry either. Ground staff never is. It's international; they've got plenty of time.

Von Werra climbed into the Hurricane. A great sense of elation seized him. A Hurricane that had just been re-fuelled! Hurriedly he examined the control panel. It was not fundamentally different from the Messer-schmitt, he decided. But – there was no sign of an auto-matic starter. Or perhaps he just couldn't identify the button? And he hadn't a parachute. 'Oh, to hell with the parachute!' he thought. 'I'll get down all right.'

The mechanic walked up and when he saw that von Werra was already in the pilot's seat he climbed on to the wing and handed the papers into the cockpit. Von Werra stuffed them into his pocket, listening to the man's talk with only half an ear, but then he heard:

'Have you signed her off?'

'What, haven't you done that?' demanded von Werra testily. 'Well, get on with it; I haven't all day to spare.'

In the meantime he had found a button that was almost certainly the self-starter. Obediently the mechanic climbed down.

'You're supposed to clear her yourself and you'll have to sign,' he called up.

'All right. All right. I'll be there in a minute.'

He waited until the mechanic had disappeared and then he pressed the button. There was a click – and silence. He tried again. Again the click. The propeller didn't move. Hurriedly von Werra searched the whole control panel. Magneto switches? There they were. He flicked them up and pressed the button again. Nothing happened. He searched desperately round the cockpit: throttle, mixture, pitch. There must be something else, some little thing . . .

Whilst his attention was concentrated on the control panel he did not notice that the Adjutant and the Duty Officer were beside the plane.

'What the devil do you think you're up to?' shouted the Adjutant.

Von Werra got a shock but he kept his head.

'It's all right, sir,' he replied cheerfully. 'Here's a machine that'll do me to get back with.'

And he had another go at the starter button.

If only the motor would start up he could pull it off even now. The Hurricane would roll off and be airborne in no time. Let them drive after him and empty their pistols at him if they liked. Once he was in the air he reckoned he could stay there come hell and high water. He waved with one hand to the two officers below whilst with the other he fiddled first with one knob and then with another in a despairing hope that at the last moment it might . . . Again and again he prodded the starter button, but the motor wouldn't budge. There wasn't a blink from it. No good; there was just some trick he didn't know about Hurricanes.

'Get out and come with me.' The Adjutant was standing on the wing now and his voice was very decided.

'Right you are, old man,' said von Werra with assumed cheerfulness and he clambered out of the cockpit. There was nothing else he could do. He saw the mechanic coming up with the papers – and, of course, a starter-battery trolley!

They all got into the Adjutant's car and drove back to the administrative building.

'We've been on the phone to your base,' said the Adjutant coldly. 'They say there's no Wellington overdue, and what's more they've never heard of you. Would you care to explain?'

'This is it,' thought von Werra. However, he tried again. Time was the thing now. If he could stall them off even for a short while he might be able to manage something.

'I can't remember your English place names,' he said. 'Perhaps I got it wrong.'

It was too feeble. The car stopped and they got out. One R.A.F. officer on one side, the other on the other. It was like a prisoner being marched off. Perhaps it was. The mess was crowded now. Everyone turned and looked at von Werra.

'Five German Luftwaffe officers escaped last night from a prisoner of war camp near Derby,' said the Adjutant.

'All over,' thought von Werra. Something must have gone wrong. They ought only just to have discovered his absence at Swanwick – and not even then if the little trick with the substitutes had worked. Perhaps the others had got caught earlier? Whatever it was, there was no point in trying to brazen it out.

'You're quite right, gentlemen,' he said. 'I am one of those five Luftwaffe officers who escaped last night. If I'd only known how to start that damned Hurricane I'd have been on my way now.'

'Your way – to where?' asked the Adjutant.

'To Dublin.'

'You would have ended up in the Irish Sea – the plane only had enough petrol for a hundred and fifty miles.'

To his enormous surprise they whooped with delight and crowded round him excitedly, shaking his hand, slapping him on the back and plying him with coffee. There was a babble of cheerful talk and admiring ejaculations. After a while, when things had calmed down a bit, he had to tell his story.

He had baled out over England on 7th September whilst giving fighter protection to a squadron of Heinkel 111 bombers. They had been attacked by Hurricanes and in the subsequent dog-fight he had collided with another machine – whether German or British he didn't know. In any case, he had stepped out. The parachute had opened safely and he made a good landing.

Von Werra was enjoying the hot drink and began to relax in the friendly atmosphere. He felt almost happy amongst these fellows. They were airmen and there was a freemasonry of the air which went beyond national boundaries – just like the freemasonry of the sea. He went on to tell them of his escape and how he had tramped through the night towards their station. He didn't tell them how he had got out of the camp – he was still cautious enough for that. Perhaps the tunnel hadn't been discovered. In that case they'd be able to use it again.

The British pilots were delighted with him and he was the hero of the hour. They looked at his uniform rather more closely and then roared with laughter at their own discomfiture. The thing was pretty obvious when you came to look into it – the badges were very primitive, hand embroidered, and not even accurate.

'He made a jolly good Dutchman though,' someone said.

'Nearly a Flying Dutchman,' said another.

'If the operator had confirmed a real telephone call – even in double Dutch – perhaps he would have been,' someone else said. And von Werra realised one trick that hadn't worked.

After a few more thumps on the shoulder it was time for them to go on duty. In the meantime arrangements had been made for taking von Werra back to Swanwick. The R.A.F. proposed to do the job and not leave it to the police. The Adjutant and two other officers went with him.

At Swanwick, after having handed him over to the Camp authorities, they parted on terms of warm friendship.

'The next time I come you must show me how to start up a Hurricane,' said von Werra as they shook hands.

'Better not perhaps, old man,' they replied. 'We'd only lose you. All the best!'

In January, 1941, Wentzel, von Werra and the other prisoners were transferred aboard the Duchess of York *to Halifax in Canada, where they entrained for Lake Superior. Von Werra, Wentzel, and a Kapitän Asmus agreed to jump from the train on the outskirts of Montreal. They planned to cross the St Lawrence River into the United States. Von Werra jumped successfully, but Wentzel and Asmus had to struggle with an iced-up window and were caught by the sentries. 'Third time's lucky,' von Werra had said as they shook hands; and after the war Wentzel pieced together, from indirect evidence, an account of that third attempt.*

Von Werra jumped in the early hours of 25th January, landing in a snowdrift. He was wearing a blue overcoat over his uniform, and a cloth cap. His story was that he was a Dutch seaman making for Ottawa, and in this guise he bluffed his way through four separate lifts, one of them in a police car. Thus he reached Prescott:

Far from looking for a warm room for himself somewhere in Prescott, von Werra was soon standing on the bank of the great river feeling very cold and looking longingly towards the far side. It was four o'clock in the afternoon, very near tea-time. The broad river ran through a flat, snow-covered landscape hereabouts, but he was unable to see the other side because it was misty and the light was already failing. As far as he could make out the surface was frozen over. He found a deserted hut in the neighbourhood and there he took shelter until it was quite dark. He didn't want anyone to see a black speck making its way from one side to the other. Cars drove along the main road which ran parallel with the river, and a horse-drawn waggon also passed, but there seemed no pedestrians, and that was a good thing. It was Saturday evening and people had long finished work and were at home.

When von Werra emerged from his hiding place to make his attempt to reach U.S. territory he bound his thick airman's scarf over his cap and ears for warmth. His overcoat and the airman's jacket and pullover beneath kept him fairly warm and in his fur-lined flying boots his feet were quite cosy. Unfortunately, however, his stomach was empty and it was twenty-four hours since he had eaten a warm meal. He now finished off his last piece of chocolate. Later he learned that the temperature had been around zero Fahrenheit that night, cold enough, but quite mild by Canadian standards for the time of year.

In any case this southern part of Ontario has the mildest climate in Canada.

First of all von Werra walked downstream a little to get away from the lights of Prescott and only then did he go down the bank to the edge of the river. By this time it was impossible to see more than twenty yards or so ahead and as he ventured out on to the ice he felt far from comfortable. However, it had to be done. How wide the river was at this point he didn't know – perhaps 500 yards, perhaps 1000, or even more. How could he be sure that he was making a bee line towards the far bank and had not perhaps started wandering up- or down-stream? There was no landmark visible on which he could have taken his bearings. Von Werra dismissed the difficulty: 'A proper flyer's born with a gyro-compass in his noddle,' he thought, and set out resolutely for the opposite bank. Fortunately there was snow on the ice, or he might have found it difficult to walk with his smooth-soled flying boots; as it was he made quite good progress. He had found a stick on shore and with this he banged the ice from time to time. It seemed as solid as a pavement under his feet and yet he had an idea that now and again he could hear the rush of water. Picking up pieces of ice that lay around on the surface he began to throw them ahead of him and listen to the sound as they fell. When they skidded along the ice with that strange eerie whirr that gradually died away he knew it was all right for him to go forward. But then one piece fell with a sudden plop into what was undoubtedly water.

Perhaps it was just a water hole left by some fisherman? Von Werra tried again with other pieces. But each piece now fell with a definite splash no matter how he varied the direction. No doubt about it, there was open water ahead. He advanced cautiously and after a while he could see it. The naval types had told him that the St Lawrence was completely frozen over at this time of the year and that he would be able to walk across. As far as the climate was concerned that was true enough, but there was a channel of water down the middle. The St Lawrence was obviously kept open for shipping by ice-breakers.

Should he try to swim across? He had trained himself with grim determination to swim for a quarter of an hour every day in the ice-cold water of the swimming bath on board the *Duchess of York* with the idea of swimming ashore, but the ship had put in to Halifax and so that had been pointless. Now it looked as though his winter-swimming training might come in useful after all. But that black, icy-cold water was intimidating and who knew how far he would have to swim? Von Werra determined to plunge into it only as a last resort. He would first try to find a boat to take him across. He therefore turned back to the Canadian shore, and, sure enough, after searching around for a while he found a boat.

It was a fairly heavy fisherman's boat and it had been drawn up on to the bank, but at least it was not chained up or fastened in any way. Inside the boat he found a piece of wood with which he tried to prise the boat loose and then he went to the stern and put his shoulder against it, getting a firm purchase with his flying boots and heaving with all his might. Before long he was sweating freely. Then the boat gave a little. And little by little he got it down on to the ice. It took him an hour's hard labour, and in the meantime he had to pause frequently, not only to rest but to make certain he would not be surprised. It would not be astonishing if the police made regular night patrols along the bank. At the first sign of danger he was ready to slip into a hollow in the snow he had discovered near by.

He had thought that he would find it easier to push the boat forward on the ice, but, in fact, it proved more difficult than before because now when he exerted his strength his feet slipped and he pushed himself away from the boat instead of pushing the boat forward. He reckoned that he had about 300 yards to go before he got to the water and at this rate it would take him all night, so he altered his tactics. Taking off his scarf he threaded it through the iron ring on the bows of the boat and the other end he looped round his chest. This imitation of the Volga boatmen did the trick and gradually he pulled the boat towards the water. Sweat was running down him from his exertions, but his face and ears were lashed by an icy wind and after a while they grew numb. Both ears were frozen during the night and for weeks afterwards he had to go around in bandages.

It was so difficult to get the boat forward that von Werra had to summon up all his strength and will-power to keep at it, and after a while he felt himself growing exhausted, and his progress, already desperately slow, grew even slower, but he gritted his teeth. It couldn't be long now. And again and again he forced himself to exert his remaining strength, straining against the tough scarf and moving the weight of the wooden boat a little further along the ice. 'I'll do it,' he muttered to himself. 'I'll do it if it's the last thing I ever do.'

He did and it wasn't.

The edge of the ice when he came to it was firm and thick; it had been shorn away by the ice-breakers that kept the channel open. It was easy to launch the boat into the water and then von Werra sprang into it and pushed off with renewed energy from the ice edge. There were no oars in the boat but there was the piece of wood he had previously found, and with this clumsy paddle he sat in the stern and propelled the boat forward across the stream to the other bank. It was impossible for him to keep a direct course now because the current was quite powerful and tended to carry the boat downstream, but he made progress. Previously he had cursed because the boat was so big and heavy; now he was glad, because large pieces of floating ice were being carried along with the current and every now and then one of them would collide violently with the boat. A frail craft would never have stood up to it and he would have found himself in the water after all.

It was slow work with his clumsy paddle and he was being carried a long way from where he had first launched the boat into the water, but that didn't worry him; no matter where he finally made land it would be U.S. territory.

The ice-free channel proved to be about 300 yards wide, but at last he was across it and the boat nosed against the thick ice of the other side. At that moment of triumph von Werra forgot his exhaustion and the cold and he sprang joyfully to his feet and leapt on to the ice. The boat bumped away behind him downstream and in his enthusiasm he began to run towards the shore, stumbling forward, but almost on wings. It couldn't be far now.

In fact he discovered that the stretch of ice on the American side was much wider than on the Canadian side and he had about 500 yards to go. He went more slowly after a while, trudging forward; for one thing he was very tired again and for another he was keeping a careful look-out. He didn't want to fall into the hands of the American police too soon. They might just put him back on the other side as the easiest way of settling the problem.

At last he reached the bank and climbed onto U.S. territory. He stood there for a moment looking round. He could have yodelled in delight, but he suppressed the impulse; he didn't feel altogether safe yet; he wanted to get further inland. At a little distance he saw a very large building with many lighted windows and cautiously he made towards it. He found that it was surrounded by iron railings and he had an idea that the windows were barred. That wasn't at all promising. Police stations, prisons and such like institutions had barred windows. More cautiously than ever he skirted the building and had a look at the front of it which was on the far side away from the river and faced onto a main motor-road which ran parallel with the St Lawrence on this side just like the one on the Canadian side.

There was a car at the entrance gates, and two women were standing near it chatting. Women are always easier to manage for a man and von Werra went up to them. After all, it was only about ten o'clock and there was nothing extraordinary about that. But at the last moment and when it was too late to draw back he saw that the bonnet of the car was raised and that a man was bending over the engine making some adjustment. As previously with the policeman therefore, von Werra went on and chanced his luck.

The women noticed at once that there was something strange about him. The tremendous efforts of the past few hours had left his face drawn and haggard and although it had not been snowing for some time his clothes were covered with slushy snow. That was because he had taken cover in snow holes from time to time for fear of being seen.

'What's the matter with you?' asked one of them, and at that moment von Werra noticed the sign over the gates. It said 'Hospital', and not 'Police Station' as he had feared. These women were perhaps nurses. He decided that frankness would be the best tactic.

'My name is von Werra,' he said. 'I am a lieutenant in the German air force and I have just escaped from Canada.'

'Well, what do you know about that!' exclaimed one of the women in vast astonishment. 'Have a cigarette.'

Von Werra was taken into police custody, freed on bail, and eventually smuggled out on a false passport via Japan, China and Russia. He was the only German officer to escape, get home and fight again. On 25th October, 1941, he was killed on the eastern front. Wentzel lived out the war and its aftermath in a series of prison camps; his attempts to escape were unsuccessful. On 3rd July, 1947, he was at last sent home from England to a devastated Germany. 'When I climbed into the train that was to take me to Berlin,' he wrote, 'I thought of my own comrades who would never come home as I was going home. The seven men of our crew who had been drowned in the Atlantic, for example. Then there were Franz von Werra and Lieutenant-Colonel von Wedel, who had returned to Berlin before me, but to die. (Von Wedel, a Luftwaffe officer in his fifties, lame, had been repatriated from prison camp in 1944 and killed in action defending Berlin against the Russian advance.)

For a moment amidst all that misery I wondered which of us had really been fortunate. But when I saw my wife waiting for me on the platform at Berlin-Grünewald, pale and thin after those seven years of parting, but with a radiant face, I no longer wondered. I knew.'

When Darkness Comes

A primitive tribe is divided by the jealous ambition of one of its members, who leaves with a band of followers. Soon both the deserters and those who stayed find that reduced numbers make survival even more precarious and Morg, the chief's son, tries to bring his people together again. The need for unity suddenly becomes vital when a horrifying new enemy appears from nowhere to threaten the very existence of the tribe.

Robert Swindells' first novel is an unusual and gripping tale for older children.

The 'Tripods' trilogy

The setting of John Christopher's outstanding trilogy is a world dominated by the Tripods, ruthless metal monsters. *The White Mountains* is the first book and it tells the exciting story of how Will Parker, his cousin Henry and their friend Beanpole make their way south to the refuge of the last free men on earth.

The second book of the trilogy. *The City of Gold and Lead*, describes how Will and his companion Fritz, now members of the resistance group in the White Mountains, are sent on a perilous mission to penetrate one of the Masters' cities. They discover who control the Tripods and make the first steps towards the final overthrow of the oppressors.

The trilogy is brought to a tremendous climax in *The Pool of Fire*, when with the aid of Will's discoveries about the Masters and their Tripods, a bold and desperate plan is formed for their overthrow. The partial failure of the first attempt leaves the world poised on the brink of disaster until the very end of this gripping and dramatic book.

More Beaver Books

We hope you have enjoyed this Beaver Book. Here are some of the other titles:

They Amazed the World A Beaver original. A collection of stories about all kinds of people whose achievements have amazed the world, from Nelson to Florence Nightingale and Einstein to Edison; fully illustrated, for readers of nine upwards

Looking at Wildlife A Beaver original. Nicholas Hammond has written an invaluable guide for young naturalists, with lots of information on all kinds of wild creatures as well as advice on the best ways of observing them. Illustrated throughout

Why Does a Glow-worm Glow? A Beaver original. Dozens of answers to intriguing questions on science topics, illustrated throughout by Mike Jackson and with a lively text by Professor Eric Laithwaite, well-known as a contributor to the BBC radio programme Dial-a-Scientist

Children of Morrow Tia and Rabbit's telepathic powers enable them to reach out from the harsh society of the future in which they live and communicate with members of a superior race. The hazardous journey they make to reach this life of freedom is the subject of an unusual and gripping story for older children by H. M. Hoover

New Beavers are published every month and if you would like the *Beaver Bulletin* – which gives all the details – please send a large stamped addressed envelope to:

Beaver Bulletin
The Hamlyn Group
Astronaut House
Feltham
Middlesex TW14 9AR

362817